LUKE DAWSON: WELLS FARGO AGENT

Other books by Denny Andrews:

Luke Dawson: Wells Fargo Gun

LUKE DAWSON: WELLS FARGO AGENT

•

Denny Andrews

AVALON BOOKS
NEW YORK

Published by Thomas Bouregy & Co., Inc.
160 Madison Avenue, New York, NY 10016

Library of Congress Cataloging-in-Publication Data

Andrews, Denny.
Luke Dawson : Wells Fargo agent / Denny Andrews.
    p.   cm.
ISBN 978-0-8034-9881-5 (acid-free paper)
I. Title.

PS3601.N55263L849   2008
813'.6—dc22   2007027262

PRINTED IN THE UNITED STATES OF AMERICA
ON ACID-FREE PAPER
BY HADDON CRAFTSMEN, BLOOMSBURG, PENNSYLVANIA

To Lorna, Denny, Sally, Bob, Tracy, Jordan, Sean, Sarah, and Max

Chapter One

Deadwood, Late July 1876

It was hot, a searing heat that dries a body out as soon as it gets wet. People and animals moved in slow motion not wanting to expend any unnecessary energy.

Luke Dawson stepped out of Number Ten Saloon into the heat and glaring sunlight and was immediately recognized.

"There you are, Dawson," boomed a voice. "I've been lookin' for you."

Reno Sinclair considered himself a bad man and he was. He'd killed several men in gunfights.

Sometimes, though not often, he'd given them an even break. This was not one of those times. He was tall with blue eyes, a brown mustache, and a scar across his right cheek. His boots were custom and his gun rig polished and well cared for.

"Well, you've found me Sinclair. What's on your mind?"

"Cletus Heppleman was a friend of mine. What do you say to that?" His back was to the sun and he had a hand wrapped around his holstered Colt single action revolver. He flipped a whiskey bottle away with his left hand. It landed without breaking and spun crazily away in the hardpacked dirt.

Luke unthonged his Colts and crossed his hands, left over right. "I'd say you weren't too choosey about your company. Cletus was a stagecoach robber and a murderer. He got what he deserved."

Luke stepped forward so his left side was facing Sinclair, making him a smaller target.

People scattered from the line of fire of the two men and lined up at a safe distance to watch. Odds were quickly being given and taken on the outcome.

"You still didn't have no reason to kill him."

"Anytime a man pulls iron on me I don't count that as a friendly act."

Luke let the situation play itself out. Like many men Sinclair had to drink and talk himself into a killing frenzy. *Maybe he'll talk himself out of it. It's happened before,* Luke thought. "Why don't you let it go Sinclair? Just walk away. And I'll walk away."

Sinclair saw his mistake in giving Luke time to prepare. He shook his stained gray Stetson. "Can't," Sinclair said and pulled his pistol, clearing the holster. Then a big weight seemed to fall on his chest. He grabbed his pistol with his left hand to help his right lift it up. The weight crushed him down. "I—ah." Sinclair fell without another breath.

Luke had pulled his Colt from the cross-draw holster but had to raise the muzzle only two inches to fire. It was so fast that many thought it was some kind of a trick. He fired three shots rapidly. Then when he saw Sinclair trying to get off a last labored shot he reluctantly fired twice more. Sinclair lay sprawled in the dust. Luke holstered his weapon and drew his other Colt with his left hand. He scanned the area to see if Cletus Heppleman had any more foolish friends. Apparently he didn't. Luke shook his head then turned around and walked back inside the Number Ten.

Money changed in the hands of the bettors. The

winners were chuckling. "The kid's fast and he's smart. Did you see the way he turned? Sinclair should have had his gun out. Even then it likely wouldn't have been close."

Chapter Two

Luke had gained a lot of experience over the previous couple of years. With the flow of gold from the Black Hills it was a lively time to catch crooks and would-be stage robbers. Whenever he deemed it necessary, he also took a job riding shotgun on the stage out of Deadwood. Johnny Slaughter was his favorite driver and always gave Luke a hair-raising ride. The criminals seemed to know when Luke was aboard and didn't bother the stagecoach no matter how much gold might be on board. Early on Luke had had frequent shooting scrapes but when the second-place finishers wound up in Boot Hill, people just naturally gave Luke a wide berth.

There were also shooting contests to take away some of the boredom. Luke generally entered these and always won. A few days later, when he was shooting a shotglass out of the air he heard a loud familiar voice say, "I think you're as good as I ever was."

Luke turned. "Jim, Wild Bill, how are you?"

In truth, time had not been kind to Wild Bill Hickok and it showed. He wore glasses much of the time, which gave him a professorial look, and his hair was streaked with gray. Although he was almost forty, his bearing was still ramrod straight.

They embraced warmly, eye to eye, pupil to mentor. "Oh, I'm getting by Luke. I got tired of all that playacting with Bill Cody's show and decided to come up here for a spell and try my luck at the turn of the cards, maybe even dig for some gold. That yellow metal's been eluding me for most of my life. Say, that was quite a shooting show you were putting on there."

"Aw, Jim." Luke was mildly embarrassed. "I'm just doing what you taught me. If people know what they're up against, they might not want to try. It works too, at least most of the time."

"So I've heard." Jim laughed. "You're getting quite a name as a man to avoid. Watch your back."

"I always sit with my back to the wall, just the way you taught me."

"Good, good. Say how are the colonel and Pete and everyone?"

"They're great. Say, let's go have some dinner, my treat. I'd like to tell you everything that's occurred the last couple of years."

As they walked over to the Senate saloon and restaurant, Jim couldn't help admiring how Luke had come to be the spitting image of his father. They talked long into the night. Luke also told Jim all about his involvement with Wells Fargo. He'd become a special agent, sent on assignments to fix company problems.

"Luke, you may be young in years, but you're a man full-growed all right. I'm right proud of the way you turned out."

"Thanks, Jim. I have you to thank for an awful lot of the way I turned out. I suppose you heard the news about General Custer."

"Yes I did Luke. It's a darn shame but he died the way he would have wanted, face front with guns in his hands."

"I guess that's right. He certainly was a leader of men. My dad had a great deal of respect for him."

"So did I, Luke. We didn't always see eye to eye, the general and I, but he was all man."

"Johnny and I have to go out on a run, Bill. I'll be back in a few days and then we can spend some more time together."

"I'd like that, Luke. See you in a few days."

Chapter Three

A few days later, August 2, Luke and Johnny Slaughter brought the stage into Deadwood at their usual fast pace, careening around corners and coming to a shuddering halt in front of the express office.

It was late afternoon. A crowd had gathered and was laughing at the antics of Francisco Mores, one of the local characters. Francisco was trying to convince the townsmen that an Indian attack was imminent. To authenticate his story, he was carrying around the severed head of an Indian. If he thought his story needed any more emphasis, he would shove the severed head into the face of the bystanders. While many thought this to be hilarious, some of them in light of the recent Custer debacle, did not.

One of the latter was a local gambler, James Pierce, who had little sense of humor and less tolerance for tomfoolery. When Francisco shoved the severed head into Pierce's face, Pierce shoved him away angrily. Delighted with this reaction, Francisco again shoved the severed head into Pierce's face. Pierce turned an angry crimson. "Do that again and so help me I'll kill you."

Francisco walked away jauntily only to return a few minutes later. He sneaked up behind Pierce and thrust the head around in front of him and into his face much to the crowd's delight.

"That's the last straw," Pierce angrily declared.

With that he drew a pistol and shot Francisco dead on the spot. The sound of the big Colt reverberated down the street, scattering the crowd and the humor with it.

"I told him," Pierce exclaimed, glaring into Francisco's sightless eyes. Then he kicked away the Indian head. "I told him."

With the show coming to its very final conclusion, the onlookers began to drift away.

One of the spectators looked up at a bemused

Luke and Johnny. "Hey, did you hear the news? Wild Bill Hickok is dead."

Stunned, Luke could only stare at the man.

Johnny looked over at an ashen-faced Luke and then back down at the man. "How?" he asked.

"Don't rightly know, exactly," the man said, scratching his chin. "I do know it was over at Number Ten Saloon. Drifter, name of Jack McCall, shot him in the back."

The next few days were a blur to Luke. He saw to the burial of Wild Bill, his mentor and friend, in the Deadwood cemetery. He also viewed with contempt the illegal miners' court acquittal, by way of bribery, of a strutting, lying Jack McCall.

A few days later, in the evening, Luke paid a visit to the hovel McCall occupied on the outside of town.

"McCall," Luke yelled out. There was no sign of movement in the tiny cabin. "McCall, I know you're in there."

The door opened a crack, McCall peered out showing only his nose and one eye. "Whatch'ya want?"

Luke stood relaxed, his hands at his sides. "I don't figure you want to face me or any man straight on. I know you're too yellow for that. Time you were movin' on. If I see you anywhere around here, I'll kill you. That's more warning than you gave Wild Bill." Luke turned and walked away.

The next day McCall was gone. When he was next heard from, McCall had been hoisted by his own petard, literally.

Luke was instrumental in bringing about the demise of McCall. He accidentally ran into McCall and watched his antics from the background.

Having bragged as a performer at a nickel side show in Laramie about killing the greatest gun ever, and how he had put one over on Deadwood, he was arrested and sent back to Yankton in the Dakota Territory. There, in Federal Court, McCall was tried, convicted and hanged in 1877.

Chapter Four

A week after running McCall out of Deadwood, Luke stopped by the Number Ten. Sitting there, playing poker was none other than John Varnes.

Varnes was a big man who thought highly of himself. He was wearing a black suit over a brocade vest, topping off his ensemble with a black Stetson. A big black cigar was clamped in his teeth.

Varnes was pontificating. "Well, I don't see why Jack had to leave town so fast, he was a nice little guy. I don't see what all the fuss was about, Hickok wasn't all that much. Why many's the time I had to stare him down over a poker hand. He was quite a card cheat you know, he wasn't all that great with a gun either." Warming to his subject, Varnes continued. "In any standup shootout, I could've taken him. He was real sneaky about the way he did things too."

Luke had heard about Varnes and knew that he was at least partly responsible for Wild Bill's death. He knew that Varnes had paid McCall, and was personally behind the bribery of the so-called jury. Shaking off the restraining hand of Johnny Slaughter, Luke put down his beer mug and sauntered over to Varnes slowly. The only way anyone could tell that Luke was upset was by looking at the back of his neck which was beet red. His eyes were a dark smoldering blue. Luke stopped two feet away from Varnes and stared down at him.

Disconcerted, Varnes looked up from his cards at Luke. "What are you staring at?"

"Your mouth," Luke answered softly.

Varnes smirked and laughed. "What about it, sonny?"

"I'm looking at it to see if a word of truth will ever come out of it instead of that lying garbage I hear spewing forth," Luke again answered softly.

Varnes threw down his cards angrily, and started to get up. Luke put an iron grip on his shoulder and said in a conversational tone, "Tell you what, Varnes, you pull a gun now, get it in your hand. I won't draw until I see the gun in your hand. Wild Bill Hickok taught me to shoot, and if you can beat me maybe you could have beaten him, instead of hiring it done."

"I ain't armed," Varnes declared sullenly.

The noise in the Number Ten had ceased, the crowd watching in eager anticipation.

Luke still was wearing his gloves from the stage run. He was standing at Varnes' left and then pivoted to his own left. Luke felt as if he was back on the ranch, cutting a stubborn batch of weeds with a backhand swing of a sickle. His movement was just as fluid, having done it thousands of times on the ranch and in training with Sing Loo. Like a spring Luke coiled up, and like a whip he unleashed his closed fist in a solid backhand swing. Luke's leather-clad fist caught Varnes on the right side of his face.

The hat stayed where it was for a moment, poised in midair, as Varnes flew off the stool and landed a few feet away on his back. He rolled over and got up on all fours then he spit out some teeth. The cigar had long since departed. The rolling teeth sounded like dice on the hardwood floor. Luke walked over and kicked Varnes in the rump. Varnes landed on his belly with a "whoosh" escaping from his shattered mouth. Grabbing a coattail in each hand, Luke ripped the coat up and off Varnes' back leaving only the sleeves on his arms.

Reaching into the leather-lined inside pockets of both the pieces of coat, Luke pulled out not one but two Remington .41 caliber double derringers. Luke kicked Varnes in the chest. His stovepipe boots made a sharp cracking sound when they connected with Varnes' ribs. Varnes again got up, slowly, on all fours, his head hanging down. Luke leaned down and placed the two derringers in front of Varnes.

Luke slowly pulled off his gloves as he spoke. "Here, Varnes, here's the guns you ain't armed with." Luke stepped back three paces. "The deal still stands, pick 'em up, cock 'em. I won't make a move until you're ready."

Varnes looked at the little Remingtons. The silence in the room was broken only by the drip-drip of blood from his mouth. Slowly, Varnes wagged his head back and forth. He didn't want to touch his guns. Luke walked behind Varnes again and kicked him in the rump. Varnes fell forward on his face, scattering the small pistols, and causing him to emit a low moan.

Luke kicked him again. "If you were half a man Varnes I'd kill you now. If I could prove any of the things I've heard, I'd kill you. But you're not anything, except lower than a snake, so crawl, go on, crawl out of here like the snake you are. Let everybody see the big brave gambler who claims to have stared down Wild Bill Hickok. Stare him down? You aren't fit enough to have licked his boots."

Most of the patrons of Number Ten were greatly amused by this spectacle. Wild Bill Hickok had been just as popular as Varnes was unpopular. Varnes was a braggart. It was no secret that he had gotten on Wild Bill's bad side and was afraid of him. The bar patrons were happy to see the humiliation of Varnes and crowded around to get a closer look.

Luke followed Varnes as he crawled through the batwing doors and kicked him again into the dust of the road. Varnes lay there unmoving. One of his torn coat sleeves had fallen off. Luke walked back inside, pocketed the two derringers and went over to the bar. The noise level was getting back to normal with a low hum.

One of the onlookers hollered, "Varnes, hey, Varnes, is that there a new fashion? One sleeve off, one sleeve on? Haw, haw. Diddle diddle dumpling, my son John."

Another spectator was peering down at Varnes' bloody face. "I didn't see nothin' comin' out of your mouth Varnes ceptin' some teeth. You shoulda kept it shut in the first place but, Lord forgive me, it was sure fun to watch."

Johnny was laughing and shaking his head as Luke walked back to the bar. "Shouldn't a' done that, Luke."

"Yeah, I know Johnny. Wild Bill would say it's better to kill him than to go to all that trouble."

"That's it exactly old son. Only now you're going to have to watch your backside more than your front."

Luke knew that Johnny was right and for the next few days did in fact watch his back wherever he went.

It was no surprise therefore, when one evening Luke spotted a rifle being aimed at him from the corner of a building he had just passed. In a blur Luke whirled, drew, and fired three times. The sounds of Luke's Colt were so close together that they blended into one long echo. One of Luke's bullets hit the rifle barrel, and the other two splintered the wood on the corner of the building on which the rifle was braced. A howl of "Ooo-wwww" filled the darkness accompanying the clatter of the dropped rifle. The sound of rapidly retreating footsteps served to put a final exclamation to the whole episode.

With no law to speak of in Deadwood, Luke himself put the word out. "I'm looking for Varnes. When I find him, I'm going to cut a piece out of him. In the meantime, if anyone even looks cross-eyed at me, I'll take care of that. Then I'll cut larger pieces out of Varnes."

Varnes disappeared. Apparently he had gotten the word, however, because no further attempts were made on Luke's life. Once, coming out of the express office, Luke spotted a man with a bandaged eye and face. The man took one look at Luke and beat a hasty retreat.

Jerome Puddington, Luke's Wells Fargo boss and mentor, had received the reports on Wild Bill Hickok's death. Knowing what Luke thought of Wild Bill, and knowing Luke, Jerome was not surprised to hear of McCall leaving Deadwood and of the public thrashing of Varnes. It was with real regret that Jerome assigned Luke out of Deadwood. Luke had done a good job but Jerome knew that to leave him there was to invite his murder. It would be only a matter of time, Luke was becoming too well known.

Luke said his good-byes to Johnny Slaughter and the rest of the Wells Fargo people in Deadwood. In truth, Luke was not sorry about leaving. The memories of that one day, August 2, were just too painful.

Chapter Five

Luke took his leave and rode back to Kansas
and his home ranch the Circle D just in time to
help with the fall roundup. Henry Bowen came
riding in a week later. There was a happy reunion.
Of course his father the colonel wanted to know
how things were going but the conversation stalled
at the mention of General Custer and then Wild
Bill Hickok.

In a somber voice, Luke recounted the events as
he knew them relating to the death of Wild Bill.
He tried to downplay the later events but Andrew
Lewis had filled the colonel in on what had happened. All the Circle D veterans of the battle with

the neighboring Bar H were gathered around listening to the conversation with rapt attention.

"I guess Jim didn't follow his own advice," the colonel observed.

"You mean about never sitting with your back to the door?" Luke asked.

"That's right."

"Wild Bill would have been the first to agree with you, Dad. He didn't have his back to the front door, it was to the side door. That's where the little coward got in."

"At any rate, it's a darn shame. Wild Bill Hickok deserved better."

"Yes, he did."

All the hands were there except John Fowler. John was in Dodge City, where he was making the acquaintance of one Gracie LeBeau, widow of the late sheriff Tom LeBeau. The good citizens of Dodge City had awarded Gracie enough money to open a millinery shop and had encouraged her to do so. They felt that if she had the gumption to stick up for herself the way she had then she could make a business succeed also, and so she did.

John hadn't had to settle for a woman as ugly as a Rogers and Spencer revolver after all. In his mind, Gracie was as beautiful as a Tiffany-engraved

Colt Navy, even though she preferred to shoot the Smith and Wesson American revolver, the same one John did.

The days went by very fast for Luke. He was glad to be back seeing not only his dad but also ranch cook Sing Loo, and hands Pete, Rowdy, Tex and John. Through Lewis, the colonel had purchased the Bar H Ranch.

Sing was still an outstanding cook. He loved to make different kinds of meals for Luke and Henry, although they were still unwilling to try his buried eggs. In the absence of Luke and Henry, John was now the steady workout partner of Sing. All four of them would again have mock fights in the barn as time permitted.

"Ever get in any scrapes in the far yonder?" John asked, looking at both Luke and Henry.

"Yeah," Henry answered. "I had to knock out a couple of miners up in Boise. They weren't armed but they sure were just cussed mean. If they'd been armed I'd have had to kill them."

"What happened? I mean how'd you do it?" John asked.

"I was just sorta' feelin' my way around Boise. I was tryin' not to attract any attention when these two jaspers started in on me. Said I looked like I was from Texas and who did I think I was? Just some more Texas trash. I tried to smile my way out of it. You know my winnin' smile?"

The Colonel, John and Luke all chuckled. Sing smiled.

"Well," Henry continued, "they just weren't the smilin' type 'cause they was havin' none of it. They were both good sized and one of 'em commenced to shove me while the other worked his way around to the back of me. Well they both had on these big old low-topped boots. I knew that if I ever got on the ground that those two would stomp me into nothin' but a wet spot in the road.

"I hauled off and kicked the one shoving me right in the shin 'bout as hard as I could. It must have hurt some because he dropped his hands down to his shin and began hollerin' somethin' awful. Then I turned and hit the second one in the bread basket with my elbow. He looked right sick and bent over gaspin' for air. I wanted to end the whole fracas so I grabbed the second feller by the collar and ran him straight into the feller still complainin' about his shin. When those two heads hit I swear you coulda heard it a mile away."

Luke, John and the colonel were laughing out loud. Sing chuckled.

"They both sorta' laid down and rested there right peaceful like. I left. Like I say though, if they'd been armed I'd have had trouble, real trouble."

"That's right," Luke said. "Most people pack iron. If they don't, they advertise the fact real loud. Of course, sometimes they lie about not being armed. When that happens, I've had occasion to knock a few fellows out too."

"Maybe make them crawl a little, in the process," the colonel added with a wry grin.

Startled, Luke glanced over at the colonel. How had his dad found out about Varnes?

Sing chimed in. "Remember, anything can be a weapon. Not just a gun or knife."

Luke smiled. "Even dung, right Sing? Or a hand used to squeeze?"

Sing smiled back. "That's right." John and Henry chuckled.

Henry and Luke would sometimes take rides together, talking shop about Wells Fargo. They both agreed that, at times, the job was the most exciting either could have ever imagined. Other times, for days even weeks on end, it could be the most boring of occupations, particularly when they were performing mundane jobs in undercover roles such as that of clerks or stable-hands.

Over the next couple of years Luke or Henry would miss the odd roundup due to pressing matters at Wells Fargo, but for the most part they were at the Circle D at least twice a year.

The Circle D continued to prosper. With the addition of the Bar H land they could run several thousand head of cattle. After fattening them up it was only a short drive to Dodge City and a good profit.

Luke spent time all over the western part of the United States for Wells Fargo, from Deadwood to San Antonio and Dodge City to San Francisco. Sometimes, he could avoid a gunfight, sometimes not. Luke's reputation continued to grow as a pretty fair gambler and a lightning-fast gun.

He managed to keep his connection to Wells Fargo a secret from almost everyone in the new towns . . .

Chapter Six

1879

The stagecoach moaned and shuddered as it came over the rise. The horses' breath exhaled short bursts of steam. It was a cold day for the run to Durango. The sky was overcast and threatened snow but the scenery was worth traveling for, at least. In the distance the mountains were resplendent under a blanket of white.

The route to Durango was treacherous in places and more like a trail than a road.

The big Concord stagecoach made the ride a little easier. Made by the Abbott, Downing and

27

Company out of Concord, New Hampshire, its thick ox-hide thorough braces gave the stage a rocking motion instead of the bone-jarring ride that it would have had with springs.

Wells Fargo had been on the route less than a year and was suffering financial trouble and bandit trouble. It wasn't only that the stages were being robbed—that was bad enough—but the bandits took great delight in robbing and humiliating the passengers; making the men, and sometimes the women, disrobe and walk into the hills while the bandits laughed, whooped it up and rode off with their loot.

Luke was keeping an eye out. *I wonder just where they could be and if they might try it?*

Luke was with three other passengers—Charles Cavendish, Red Barker, and Miss Laura Jensen.

Beside Luke was Cavendish, a portly banker in his mid-fifties. Cavendish was shorter than Luke at five and a half feet but he outweighed him by twenty pounds. Cavendish's black three-piece suit, bow tie, and shoes were set off by a large gold watch chain across his ample front. Like Luke, he also wore a Stetson hat but with a narrow brim.

Across from Luke sat Barker, a drummer. At best, Barker could be called unkempt. His loud plaid suit did not fit him and his red hair stuck out in tufts under the small bowler hat which perched awkwardly on his head. Barker was a burly man in his thirties, about five foot nine. While his hands were callused from hard work, he was already showing signs of a paunch from a dissipated lifestyle. His blood-shot eyes, boozy breath, and three-day growth of beard did nothing to improve his appearance. While Barker seemed convincing as a whiskey peddler, clearly he'd been sampling his own wares. There was something about him that didn't fit.

Next to Barker sat Laura. She wore a long blue dress with a starched white collar. To shield herself from the dust, she wore a scarf and a light colored duster. She was a pretty blond, blue-eyed, and about five-foot-five with a direct look, but that was all anyone knew.

No matter how hard Barker tried he couldn't draw her out. "Where you from missy?" Later he asked, "You going to stay in Durango missy?" After a while he gave up in disgust.

Luke folded his arms and sat back to watch the chiseled peaks of the countryside pass.

Up topside was Bill Ryan, the jehu or driver, and Horace Gates riding shotgun.

Both were thickset men and had ridden together over different routes for four years. They had been held up twice—the last time they were run into the trees in just their longjohns. They were not happy. Today, with $20,000 in gold coin on board, they were understandably nervous.

Bill was in his forties and he couldn't remember a time when he wasn't driving a conveyance of some sort. He loved driving and at five-foot-ten and over two hundred pounds was well suited for it. His thick arms and sturdy legs could handle the big stage through the most difficult situations.

Over four years in the Civil War he'd driven for the Excelsior Brigade in the Union Army. Hauling ordnance of all kinds hadn't fazed Bill. It was when he had to haul full barrels of gunpowder under hostile fire that he sweated a mite. *Nothing,* Bill thought, *could be as bad as being shot at and driving a load of gunpowder. I reckon those bandits are around though. I'd sure hate to run through the woods again.*

Luke was shaken out of his reverie by the drunken taunt of Barker. "Hey there little miss high and mighty, you won't be so uppity if we get held up. In fact, I'm looking forward to running after you in the woods with nothing on, haw haw haw."

Laura paled, but said nothing.

"See here," said Cavendish, "that's no way to talk to a lady."

"Aw, shut up, fat man. I'll talk any way I want. Besides I ain't so sure she's much of a lady."

Luke fixed Barker with a stare. "That's enough," he said.

"Well, now, just who do you think—"

"I said that's enough."

Barker tried to stare Luke down but it didn't work. Instead, he retreated into a sullen silence. Laura glanced gratefully at Luke and Cavendish then looked out the window. The stage was traveling at a fast pace, almost seven miles an hour.

Luke took a renewed interest in Barker, trying to figure what it was that didn't fit about him. *Of course, it's the shoes, or rather, not the shoes.* Barker didn't wear shoes or even brogans, but boots. True, his pants were pulled over them, but boots they were—scuffed, down-at-the-heel boots, at that. They didn't go with Barker's loud ill-fitting drummer suit. Luke wondered what the origins of the suit and Barker really were. He didn't have long to wait to find out.

Chapter Seven

The stage slowed for a bend in the road. Suddenly, out of the trees rode three men. There was no doubt about what they intended to do. They were wearing dusters and long black hoods with eye and mouth holes.

"Throw down that scattergun or I'll scatter you all over and have fun doing it," said the first hooded man to Horace. He was holding a double barrel 10 gauge Greener shotgun, the business end of which looked as big as a cannon.

"You're nothin' but a pack of lowlifes," Horace said.

"Watch it! Is that the only gun you've got?"

"Yeah, just like last time," Horace lied. Then Horace threw his own shortened "stagecoach" shotgun down on the ground.

Luke had already flicked the rawhide thongs off the hammers of his Colts. He looked up, straight into the twin barrels of a Remington .41-caliber derringer held by a smirking Barker. The little gun was deadly at under ten feet.

"Don't be pulling them hoglegs. We'll hear what the nice men have to say, then be on our way." Barker laughed.

Cavendish, frozen in fear, could only say, "Oh nooo."

From an unexpected quarter came help in the form of a handbag—Laura's handbag. A very angry and red-faced Laura rared back and hit Barker full in the face with it, stinging him and blocking his vision.

At the same instant, Luke grabbed the derringer, twisting it up and blocking the hammer from firing with his finger. Simultaneously, Luke drew his own pistol and slammed it into Barker's skull. Barker's eyes started to roll back in his head. His bowler hat tumbled off to the side with a large crease in it. Luke flipped the derringer to Laura, who caught it deftly. Then he grabbed Barker by the collar and shook him viciously.

"Don't you pass out, blast you." Luke shook Barker again and said, "Come on, we'll see what the 'nice men' have to say to you." Barker's head bobbed back and forth as if it was independent of his neck.

From outside the stagecoach came the voice of the second bandit. "All right, throw down the box and you passengers get out. Now, let's see what kind of fun we're going to have here today."

Luke held onto Barker's collar and twisted it with his left hand, keeping him close. Although Barker's eyes were clearing a little, he was still groggy and subdued. Since the ruckus had taken place on the other side of the stagecoach it had been outside the bandits' vision.

"When the shooting starts, Charles, you and Laura get down and out of the other side of the stage if you can," Luke said quietly. They both nodded silently.

Luke held his Colt in the small of Barker's back. With his left hand gripping his collar, Luke half-walked and half carried Barker past Laura and Cavendish and off the stage.

Horace had lifted the dark green strongbox to the edge of the stage, then looked down and saw what Luke was doing. He delayed throwing the treasure box to see what would happen next.

The second bandit, in the middle, was holding a rifle. He blinked when he saw Barker's bright hair standing out like a beacon and said, "Hey, Red's not supposed to get off first, something's funny. In fact, Red looks downright funny." Barker was wobbling while he tried to stay upright in Luke's iron grip.

The third bandit, the biggest of the three and holding a pistol, said, "Shut up, you fool."

Seeing the first bandit with the shotgun as the biggest threat, Luke went after him.

He brought his Colt from behind Barker's back. The snick-snick sound of the hammer being cocked was unusually loud in the cold fall afternoon. Taking a swift, sure aim, Luke fired but the bandit never heard it. He spilled out of the saddle, dead, with the duster and the hood twisted around, looking like a clump of last week's laundry.

The second bandit, with the rifle, leveled it down on Luke. But Red was in the way. *Oh, well, too bad for Red,* he thought.

"No, no, no, no, don't shoot, Charlie," Barker said.

From topside of the coach, Horace pulled out an Army pistol that had been converted from percussion to cartridge. He had it hidden inside his mackinaw, in a shoulder rig. Taking what cover he could behind the express box, he fired at the bandit with the rifle and spoiled his aim at Luke. The bandit adjusted his aim, and fired at Horace. The rifle bullet made a whining sound as it ricocheted off the metal edge of the box.

Luke dropped the blubbering Barker and drew with his left hand, even as he was firing with his right. Two of Luke's slugs went crashing into the second bandit's chest. With a cry, the bandit threw the rifle in the air and collapsed onto the ground. Blood seeped out of the hood. The horses reared up at the gunshots, hooves flailing in the air, to add further to the confusion.

What should have been easy pickings with Barker on the inside, was not working out that way at all. In the melee, the third bandit fired a couple of desultory shots from his pistol then skedaddled, zigzagging to make a more difficult target. Luke emptied both of his pistols at the fleeing bandit. He saw him flinch at about one hundred yards away but wasn't sure if he hit him. The gunsmoke hung in the air, an acrid black powder smell.

One horse galloped off after the bandit, the other one stopped about eighty yards away. Luke walked slowly toward the horse, a dun, and talked softly. "Easy there, big fella. Just take it easy."

The big dun tossed its head and moved a few more yards off, eyeing Luke warily. Finally, it allowed Luke to take the reins. "That's a good boy, good boy. Here we go." Luke mounted the horse and trotted slowly back to the waiting stage.

Horace and Bill, who had retrieved their shotgun, were covering an indignant Barker, along with Laura, who was holding Barker's derringer.

"I ain't done nothin'," Barker whined. "I almost got killed my own self thanks to that crazy cowboy."

"You've got some explaining to do, Barker," Luke said as he rode up. "That's the only reason I don't hang you right here. Now turn around. Bill, toss me a piece of rope from up there."

All the bluster had left Barker. Within a minute he was trussed up like a chicken waiting for the axe.

"Horace, Bill, help me lash this critter up topside. I'll fashion a hangman's noose for him so if he gets all full of vinegar he won't get more than two feet away."

Bill and Horace guffawed at his rough humor. With two men dead and talk of strangling a third, the whole situation·seemed hilarious to them because they had avoided running into the woods in their underwear, or worse. However, Laura and Cavendish were both deadly serious.

"I think hanging's a good idea," Laura said.

"So do I!" Cavendish exclaimed. "Maybe we ought to string Red up right now."

Luke looked up at Barker, who was tied down with a hangman's rope tight around his neck. "You see what the sentiments of decent people are, Red? You'd better get ready to talk."

Luke went about gathering up the shotgun and the rifle along with the sidearms of the dead men and put them in the coach. They lashed the dead men to the back of the luggage carrier. Then he tied the riderless horse to the back of the stage and they set out again for Durango.

"Hiyup there!" Bill yelled.

Chapter Eight

The stagecoach creaked and clattered as it started on its way.

"Mister, I can't thank you enough!" Charles Cavendish boomed in a relieved voice. "I've heard of shooting like yours but never thought it possible before today. They are just about ready to call Durango a town and my partners and I want to get in at the start in developing the land and banking. This twenty thousand dollars is just the beginning of our investments. Why, mining activity alone will take all that, and then some."

"Oh, yes," Laura said. "Thank you so much for ridding us of those bandits. I'm sorry if I seemed standoffish before now, I've been so worried about my father."

"What's wrong?" Luke and Cavendish asked together.

"After mom died, my dad decided he couldn't farm anymore. It reminded him too much of her. He sold the farm in Missouri and we moved to Abilene. He opened a drygoods store and I taught school. When he heard about the silver and gold strikes around Leadville he got restless, he had to go. He left me in charge of the store and went to Leadville. From there he went to Animus City and staked a claim a little north of there. I had several letters from him. Apparently, he hit a good strike. First he hit silver, then a little farther in, gold.

"In the beginning, he wanted me to come down to Animus City, I guess they call it Durango now. However, in his last letter he told me to wait, that he would get in touch with me when it was safe!" Laura held back the tears.

"How long since you heard from him?" Luke asked.

"Two months," Laura said softly.

"How often had you heard from him before that?" Cavendish asked.

"Oh, at least every two weeks sometimes every week."

Cavendish and Luke glanced at each other in silent understanding and concern. The swaying of the stagecoach gave each of them time to collect his thoughts.

Luke remembered his mother taken from him when he was only five. His dad, the colonel, came to mind and his friend Jim Hickok. He thought about his first dramatic meeting with Sing Loo and all that Sing had taught him.

He chuckled to himself when he remembered the Slonikers and Henry Bowen in Dodge City and his first meeting with Jerome and Wells Fargo.

His brow furrowed when he recalled the epic battle with the Bar H. Luke's reputation with a gun began after his showdown with George Sly, the snarling cocky gunfighter.

Luke gave a little grunt and a slight shake of his head as he thought about John Fowler. First he was an enemy and now a close friend.

Finally he thought about Dick Hawthorne, the owner of the Bar H with a sideline as a robber and murderer. It was in returning his stolen money to Wells Fargo that Luke's career had been launched.

He'd come a long way in a short time.

Chapter Nine

Although it wouldn't be officially named Durango for another year, Animus City was already being called Durango. It was nestled in the San Juan Mountains twenty miles north of the New Mexico border, just east of the Animus River and named after Durango, Mexico, which means "water town." Durango was a thriving town of three hundred boasting a post office, newspaper, hotel, blacksmith, sheriff's office and jail, general store and, of course, saloons.

Luke's assignment to Durango was no particular surprise to him. He had heard about the stage robberies, of course. Luke thought it was a lucky break for him and for Wells Fargo, that his particular stage had been chosen by the bandits to be held up.

The last leg from Alamosa through the San Juan Mountain range had been a pleasant one. It was about ten miles beyond the old Anasazi Indian ruins where they had run into the bandits. Luke surmised that since bandits were basically lazy, not wanting to ride too far, they were likely headquartered out of Durango.

The planting of Red Barker on the stage to aid in the holdup however, showed sophistication and perhaps some inside contacts that most outlaw organizations didn't possess. He would have to do some looking around when they pulled in.

Of course, Luke thought wryly, sophistication isn't the term that came to mind when he thought about Barker. Barker might prove to be the weak link in the whole chain of events, weak enough to give them some information.

Luke admired Laura. In coming out here alone to look for her father she had shown some spunk. Clobbering Barker with the handbag had also taken some gumption and, Luke admitted to himself, had saved his bacon. He would like to be of some help in finding her father, though from the look of it that didn't seem promising.

On further introspection, Luke also admitted to

himself that Laura was rather pleasing to the eye. He shook his head. Oh he had a job to do but the thought of her lingered. Charles Cavendish was probably just what he appeared to be, a prosperous businessman looking for further opportunity.

The big Concord stage clattered into Durango and stopped in front of the sheriff's office. The sheriff, Caleb McCracken, walked out the door—it was unusual for the stage not to proceed on to the express office. Caleb was in his late forties, his brown hair was streaked with gray, his eyes a light blue. He had a worldly wise look. Caleb was a big man, almost as big as Pete Ryan of the Circle D. In fact, it was his size that Caleb relied upon to keep the peace. Most people, drunks or otherwise, didn't want to risk getting hit by those big ham-sized fists. Since most of his job was walking, he wore low-heeled miner's boots instead of the custom cowboy variety. His shirt was red flannel covered by a leather vest with pockets filled with 10 gauge shotgun shells. Although he carried a Colt .44–40 single action pistol low on his right hip, it was mostly for show. Caleb knew he was no hand with a six-gun. So he carried a Butler shotgun with the barrels cut down to sixteen inches. People knew to duck for cover whenever Caleb was talking seriously to someone, the quick spread of buckshot was fearsome.

Caleb looked up at the men. "Howdy, Bill, Horace, what's going on?"

"We got a special cargo for you, Sheriff," Bill said while swinging down from the stage.

Horace got down from the other side and walked around to the luggage carrier. He took out a big clasp knife and cut the ropes holding the two dead bandits, who tumbled into the street. "Yeah, I don't think they planned on being the cargo but here they are."

Luke climbed up on the stage with one easy pull and untied the hangman's rope on Red Barker. He then rolled Barker, still tied up, off the stage. Barker yelled then hit the ground with a thud, a howl, and then a groan. "Here's some more cargo for you, Sheriff. This one might even talk with a little persuasion."

Caleb's forehead wrinkled and his eyebrows shot up as if someone had just dropped snow down the back of his neck. Bill and Horace were both laughing. "I know what you're thinking Caleb," Horace said. "But believe me, this here polecat deserves every bit of rough treatment he gets."

"That's right, Sheriff," Bill said. "And if'n it hadn't been for that there young fella, we'd all be in the country in our longjohns or worse."

Cavendish and Laura got off the stage. "Never

seen anything like it, Sheriff," Cavendish told Caleb. "I mean, I've seen trick shots but never anything like what that boy did."

Caleb looked at Luke, who had bounded off the stage, and took in his gun rig, sizing him up. "You pretty fast?"

Luke didn't care for the question, but understood why the sheriff asked. "Fast enough."

"Make a habit of it?"

"Only when I can't avoid it." Luke answered.

Caleb nodded his head, satisfied at what he saw and what he heard. A small crowd of onlookers had gathered. One of them, a drummer, saw Barker being pulled to his feet by Horace. "Hey, that's my suit. That was in my luggage when it was stolen in that stage robbery two months ago."

"How can you be sure?" Caleb asked.

"Look inside at the label, it'll say, 'The Emporium, St. Louis.'"

The sheriff undid the ropes holding Barker and pulled out the front of the coat. "Sure enough, that's the label just like you said."

Barker said with a wheeze, "I bought this here suit."

"Sure you did," Caleb said, "that's why it fits so well."

Caleb pushed Barker in front of him into the office and into the back of the two jail cells. Everyone from the stage came inside and the story of the robbery and subsequent gunfight unfolded.

"I'd say you folks were right fortunate at the way things turned out," Caleb said.

"Say, isn't there a reward for fellows who rob the stage?" Luke asked.

"That's right," Caleb answered. "Five hundred dollars each, dead or alive, from Wells Fargo. It looks like you got a real windfall young fellow."

"We all did. I'd like it split five ways."

Amid a chorus of protests, Luke stood firm. "Each of you played a part in getting those bandits," Luke said, stretching the truth only a little. "The fact is that if they hadn't had some distractions it could have gone very badly for us."

"Well," Cavendish said, "I'm here to do some business, so if any of you want to set up an account, I'll be happy to take care of it. For openers, I'll donate my three hundred dollars back into the pool. You each get seventy-five more." Cavendish held up a hand. "Don't interrupt me Luke. I'm a lot older and uglier than you." Everyone chuckled. "I just want you to know how much my partners and I appreciate your actions, any time you need something, you just name it."

"Maybe put up a five hundred dollar reward for

the whereabouts of Lars Jensen," Luke suggested.

Laura looked over hopefully, "Oh, that would be wonderful." Caleb's eyebrows wrinkled again. Laura told Caleb the story of her missing father.

"I met Lars, and come to think of it I haven't seen him around here for a couple months. That's not so unusual though, they can send out for supplies. There's always haulers willing to make extra money, good money at that."

"Maybe the reward will help some memories along," Cavendish added. "We'll do it."

Caleb had the two bodies removed to the undertakers. "That one jasper was Charlie Clinton, sort of an amiable fellow but not too bright."

Horace spoke up. "That's what Red called him, Charlie."

Luke laughed. "I think that's when Red woke up. He was real anxious that Charlie not put a hole in him. If it hadn't been for Horace slinging lead at him, we might all have had some holes." Horace smiled at Luke.

"What about the other bandit, Sheriff?" Luke asked. "Have you seen him around town at all?"

"Call me Caleb, Luke. No, I haven't seen that one around here, doesn't mean that he hasn't been here though. I'll have some of the local folk take a look after the undertaker gets him ready. They'll love it, like going to a sideshow without having to pay." Everyone chuckled at the dark humor.

"Say Caleb," Luke said, "I see you've got a shortened shotgun, how would you like to have this regular length Greener I took from the bandits?"

"I'd appreciate that, I'll put it in the rack. It just may come in handy. Say, Luke, after you get situated here I'd like to have a talk with you."

"Sounds good to me. I'll be over after breakfast tomorrow morning. Is that soon enough?"

"That'll be fine."

Chapter Ten

Horace and Bill took Laura, Cavendish and Luke over to the Lincoln, a boardinghouse, not far from the center of Durango. The owner, Mrs. Cray, a feisty widow, was happy to have the extra business.

The next day, after a breakfast of steak and eggs, Luke walked over to the sheriff's office. Caleb, sitting in a big swivel chair doing some paperwork, looked up and smiled. "Hi Luke, thanks for coming over."

"Glad to Caleb." In truth, Luke had been curious what this was all about. Caleb looked him over carefully.

"Luke, I'd like to ask you a few questions, okay?"

"Shoot."

"You ever hear of a fellow named George Sly?"

Lukes eyes turned a dark steel blue. "Yep. In fact, I killed him."

Caleb nodded. "Then it was you who led the fight of the Circle D against the Bar H over there in Kansas?"

Luke exhaled a sigh. "Yes, that's right. What's this all about, Sheriff?"

"It's still Caleb, Luke. Here's the situation. I have a few part-time deputies when it's Saturday night or if I'm to be out of town. I want you to know that I intended to offer you the job of permanent deputy even before I put all of this together. Now that I have put it together I'd still like to offer you the job but I'll understand if you want to refuse it."

"Why's that?"

"You have a reputation, Luke. Some men will come running just to look at you and see not necessarily how tough you are but how tough they are."

"I've met a few like that. It doesn't usually come to gunplay but it could though. I've never worn a badge before."

"I'd like you to wear one now. The pay is fifty dollars a month and found."

"Thanks, Caleb. I'll take the job. One of the first things I'd like to do is to see if I can find out about Laura's dad."

"That's fine. Go on patrol with me, become a presence here, then nose around all you want. I'll back you." Caleb stood up and stretched his massive frame.

Red Barker started yelling from his cell in back. "Hey, Sheriff, when you gonna turn me loose? You ain't got no call to hold me."

Luke ambled back to the cell and Barker's eyes got wide as he took in first Luke and then his star.

"Don't I look just like something out of a drunken nightmare, Red? It's funny how you knew old Charlie Clinton's name. Who put the whole thing together? It sure wasn't you, you're dumber than a stump."

"I can't—I ain't sayin' nothin'." Barker turned a sickly pale, making the black and blue on the left side of his face stand out in contrast to the rest of him.

"Red," Luke said in a reasonable tone, "your so-called friends already know what you haven't figured out yet, namely that you could face the hangman. At the very least you could face a long stretch in prison. When you get out all those good looks of yours will be gone." Caleb laughed, and

Barker scowled. "Look at it this way, Red, wouldn't it be better for them if you left here feet first? Of course we'll protect you as best we can, but you may not make it through the trial." Luke turned and followed Caleb down the small hallway into the office.

"That'll give him something to chew on," Caleb growled. "You know Luke, for never having put on a badge, you sure seem to know this kind of work."

Luke gave a small smile. "Didn't say I hadn't done this kind of work, said I'd never worn a badge before." Caleb nodded thoughtfully.

The next few days went by uneventfully. Luke had talked to Laura and got all the information he could about her father. Laura was impressed with Luke's new position. "You just seem made for that job, Luke. I'm so happy for you."

"Thanks." Somehow he felt tongue-tied around Laura.

Chapter Eleven

Durango was a wide open town at its birth in 1879. Cattle was a big industry which fed the miners. The gold and silver from the mining industry in turn fed the rest of the area including the saloons, gamblers and general hangers-on. A big event was coming up, a prizefight. Fights were outlawed in many jurisdictions but Durango had no such reluctance. Particularly preferable viewing were gouged eyes and chewed ears accompanied by lots of blood.

One of the miners was the local champion, a big fellow named Bob Cromwell. Bob stood about six-foot-four and weighed two hundred and sixty pounds. Swinging a pick and sledgehammer had given Cromwell a highly developed upper body. Several ring matches and local scrapes had been of short duration and always ended in his favor. He fancied himself a tough man and, when he wasn't in the mines, he basked in the local hero worship.

Coming in against Cromwell was a relative unknown in the Durango area, Jem Riley. Jem stood six-foot-two and weighed two hundred and thirty pounds. He was by no means as big as Cromwell but he was solid. His face reminded Luke of John Fowler. Clearly, this man had had a lot of ring experience, not just in local brawls. The most curious thing about Riley was his head—his skull was thick and shaved, leaving him totally bald.

Why would anyone do that to himself? Luke knew it could get cold in Durango and that bald head wouldn't be warm.

Riley walked around town enough to be seen by the locals but carefully avoided any place where Cromwell might be. Caleb, being one of the most respected men in town, as well as one of the biggest, was hired to be the referee. The promoter of the fight was the owner of the Lucky Dog Saloon, Eddie Roe. The Lucky Dog was bigger and a cut above the other saloons in Durango. Roe thought the fight would bring in a lot of new business and sell a lot of booze. He was right on both counts.

Caleb and Luke were walking down the main street when approaching them was Riley and another big man. He wore the usual gambler's attire but sported a full beard. "Sheriff, meet Jem Riley, you'll be seeing him soon enough in the ring but I thought it best if you met him first."

Caleb shook hands with Riley. Luke noticed that the man had called Caleb, Sheriff, not Caleb. There was no easy familiarity between the two and Caleb seemed a bit stiff. Caleb introduced Luke. "Varnes, this is my new deputy, Luke Dawson."

Varnes? Luke's eyes got wide. *I didn't recognize you with that full beard.* Varnes held his hand out but Luke kept his arms folded. Varnes got a hard look in his eye and let his hand drop. "Luke and I had a misunderstanding up in Deadwood. I thought we'd let bygones be bygones."

"That was no misunderstanding Varnes. I'd sooner shake hands with a rattler. At least with a rattler you know when he's going to strike, he gives a warning."

"I had nothing to do with the death of Wild Bill Hickok," Varnes protested.

"You mean the murder, don't you? You're still wanted for questioning up in Dakota Territory."

Varnes smiled, exposing some gold teeth. "Well, I don't reckon little Jack McCall is going to be doing much talking about it, do you?"

"Not since he stretched that rope back in '77, I don't. I'm pretty sure you did see him though. I wonder how much you had to pay his family to keep him quiet."

Varnes was giving Luke a poisonous look now. "Don't know about that Dawson but I do know and remember a few things, there'll be a settling up."

Riley, giving Luke a hard look, interjected. "I'd kill a man before I let him talk to me that way."

Luke turned to Riley. "You want in on this? Go get a gun." Riley said nothing. "Don't expect any help from this yellow cur.

"Tell everyone how you happened to need all those gold teeth, Varnes. I imagine that full beard is to hide the scars on your right cheek. We'll be posting a firearms ordinance soon. When we do you'll be the first one I come to search, just like before. You still lie about a couple of little hideout guns in leather-lined pockets Varnes? That's just your style."

Humiliated by the tongue-lashing, and avoiding the curious stares of onlookers, Varnes whirled and walked away followed by Riley. They talked to each other in low angry tones.

Caleb laughed. "You just make friends everywhere you go, don't you Luke?"

Luke was still simmering. "Caleb, I've killed a lot of men who weren't as mean and cowardly as that one."

"I always suspected that Varnes had a mean streak in him but it didn't show up until today. You must have really put a whupping on him up in Deadwood."

"Yeah, and to tell you the truth Caleb, I gave him little or no chance to defend himself. I was sure he was behind the murder of Wild Bill, I still am. What's his position here locally?"

"He owns one of the two smelters here and has a few small mining claims. He gambles some and dabbles in a few other things. Frankly, as you probably guessed, I don't like the man, never have."

"So it seemed, but remember Caleb, don't turn your back on Varnes or any of his hirelings. That's how they got Wild Bill and he was the best man I ever saw with a gun."

Laura Jensen had witnessed the last part of the encounter with Varnes. She was puzzled as she walked up to Luke and Caleb. "What was all that about, Luke?"

Luke was embarrassed that she had seen the altercation. "Aw, nothing much Laura. Just a continuation of an old argument."

"Well, I must tell you, I met Mr. Varnes yesterday and he wants to help me. He seemed very concerned about my father."

"Could it be because your father has a claim somewhere and Varnes would like to find it?" Luke retorted angrily.

In a huff, Laura turned and left. Caleb's eyes were crinkled up and he was trying, unsuccessfully, to suppress a chuckle.

Luke looked at Caleb. "What'd I say?"

Caleb was still chuckling. "Luke, Luke, Luke you're as good a deputy as I've ever seen but you don't know beans about women."

"I guess not."

"Give it a day or two. Maybe she'll come to her senses and see Varnes for what he is."

"I hope so."

Four days later Luke was coming out of the mining claims office. He had been checking on the claim filed by Lars Jensen. Everything appeared in order which made him all the more suspicious of Varnes. Laura was walking in as Luke was walking out and Luke tipped his hat.

"Why Luke, are–are you still checking about my father?"

"Of course I am, Laura, you don't think I'd stop just because of that tiff the other day, do you?"

"Well, I don't know. Mr. Varnes said that you were only doing it to get in good with me, or maybe to steal my father's claim."

"What else did Mr. Varnes say?"

"He told me about how you had him held by two men while you beat him in Deadwood. That's why he had to grow that beard. He said that you think he had something to do with Wild Bill's death and you're wrong."

"Anything else?"

"No, that's about it."

"Laura, you haven't known me very long but let me ask you—do you think I would ever have a man hold another man, while I beat him?"

Laura shook her head.

"If I were hungry for money would I have split the rewards instead of keeping it all?"

Again Laura shook her head.

"Then how could you believe that Varnes is anything but a liar?"

"I wasn't sure what to believe Luke. Then when you implied that Mr. Varnes was only interested in me for my father's claim, well, no woman would want to believe that."

In spite of himself, Luke chuckled. Laura's eyes blazed, challenging his reaction. Luke held both his hands out in front of him as if to ward her off. "Caleb told me I didn't know beans about women-folk and he's right. Sure, I've seen a few women in my time but never one as nice, pretty, spirited and smart as you. Why, if it hadn't been for you swing-ing that handbag we might never have made it here. I'll take anything any man wants to offer, but when it comes to you, I–I just don't know how to talk to you. I get all sweaty and my tongue gets tied up in knots and I can't see straight."

In spite of herself, Laura smiled. "Well you cer-tainly don't seem to be having any trouble talking now Luke Dawson."

Luke smiled back, warmly. "I figured it might be my last chance. Anyone like you, well, you're going to have more marriage proposals than the Lucky Dog has whiskey bottles. I–I just want you to know I'm around." Luke was feeling foolish again.

Laura could tell the way Luke was feeling. While she didn't want to let him off the hook, she also knew that she had some deep feelings for this big deputy. What Luke didn't realize, and that

Laura would never tell him, was by his very self-effacement he was endearing himself to her in a way no one else ever could. Laura looked up at Luke, her blue eyes shining, her face framed by her blond hair. "Would you like to have supper tonight with me, Luke?"

Luke thought his hearing was going bad. "Supper?" he croaked. "Why sure, yes, I mean I'd love to. I'll meet you back at the Lincoln at six and we'll go out from there."

Laura looked intently at Luke. In some corner of her mind she was coming to a realization about him. She smiled. "I'll see you then." Without another word she walked into the mining office.

Chapter Twelve

The fall day had taken on a glow for Luke—the frost still on the street seemed like diamonds and a warm feeling coursed through him. Luke felt that he was walking on a cloud, all thoughts of his job were far from his mind. Until he was brought back to earth by a man standing in the middle of the street, arms at his sides, looking at Luke intently. Three paces farther back and about ten paces off to the right, stood a second man who was also staring stonily at Luke.

"Hey there, Depuuuty. I hear you're a reeeel bad man. I hear you're going to take our guns and spank us. That right?"

Luke knew the type he was facing, he'd seen it before. "There's a firearms ordinance coming, and when it does I'll take your guns."

The first man was dressed like a cowboy, the second man more like an undertaker—everything black including his fingernails. The contrast in garb mattered little however. They both had the same look, professional and deadly.

"Well, I'll tell you what," the first man said. "There don't have to be no wait for no ordinance, why don't we find out if you're man enough to take my gun away, right now?"

Luke saw the setup, it was well planned. The second man would draw first and fire, at least distracting and maybe hitting Luke. While Luke drew on the second man, the first would have his gun in action. Fair, no, but effective because the second man would have faded out of the picture by the time the excitement was over.

Laura had seen the two-on-one gambit before, in Abilene. She walked out of the mining office and turned left down the boardwalk, stopping just so Luke could see her out of the corner of his eye. Her blue dress stood out against the drab building, her shoulders covered by a black wool shawl. She was fumbling in her handbag.

Oblivious of Laura, the first man continued.

"What's the matter Depuuuty? You're supposed to be tough."

"What about your friend over there?" Luke asked, playing for time. "The way he's dressed, I guess he's here to bury you." Luke's blood was starting to sing in anticipation of combat.

"Who, him?" The first man gestured over his shoulder. "Don't even know his name."

"Well, go ahead then. Start all the trouble you think you can handle."

But Laura preempted the play.

She pulled out the little .41-caliber derringer, Barker's gun, and fired it not at the first man but at the second, who already had his hand wrapped around his pistol butt. The sharp crack of the little gun and the whizzing of the slug over his head were just enough to make him flinch. It was all the time Luke needed. Hands crossed left over right, Luke swung into action at the sound of Laura's pistol. Rather than just draw one gun, Luke drew both of his Colts. His .44–40 single actions sounded as one with a deep roar in the enclosed street. He fired at two targets simultaneously—the second man's pistol almost cleared leather, the first man's gun didn't make it halfway out of the holster.

Both took two bullets in the chest and were dead before they hit the ground. Their expressions were a mixture of surprise and wonderment.

Luke quickly ran over to Laura. "Are you all right?"

Laura was shaking. "I–I've never shot at a man before. I've seen men do that though"—gesturing at the two lifeless forms far apart—"I knew what they were going to do. One would try to distract you and the other would shoot and then run while the first one shot. I had to do something."

Luke was smiling and shaking his head. "That's the second time you've saved my bacon. I surely do appreciate it. It's funny though, even if you had hit him with that popgun, at that distance it might have only made him mad. As it was, you threw off their timing just a hair. And it was just long enough. Laura you're someone to ride the river with. I don't know if I'm worthy of you but I'd sure like to be considered."

Laura's eyes shone as she reached out and put a hand on Luke's forearm.

Caleb came huffing and puffing on the run. "What happened?"

Luke was filling Caleb in as John Varnes came stalking up and put out his hand to grab Laura by the shoulder. "That was a foolish thing to do, Laura, you could have gotten hurt, badly."

Luke casually reached out and took Varnes' hand

in an iron grip. He bent the hand out and back, and with a cry Varnes went down on his knees. "Varnes, If I see you anywhere near this lady you're going to get hurt, badly, get my meaning?" Luke let go of Varnes' hand.

Varnes got up, rubbing his wrist and hand, and stared at Laura. "So that's the way it is, Laura?" Laura, saying nothing, stared back steadily.

Caleb looked at Varnes. "You happened on the scene pretty quick, Varnes. You just happen to be around? Maybe you know those two jaspers from somewheres else?"

"I never saw 'em before."

"Durango isn't a very big town, Varnes," Luke said in a low conversational tone. "Suppose I happen to find out that you were seen drinking with those two?"

"Wouldn't mean a thing," Varnes said, as a nervous sweat started to appear on his forehead in spite of the cold. "Why, I'm a sociable fellow. I buy drinks all the time for fellows I don't know." Not liking the way the conversation was going, Varnes turned around and beat a hasty retreat with as much dignity as he could muster while he was still rubbing his wrist.

Caleb walked over to look at the two dead men. Luke walked a shaken Laura back into the mining office to sit, then joined Caleb. "Ever see 'em before?" Luke asked.

Caleb shook his head. "You?"

Luke shook his head. "Maybe they were brought in from out of town to knock out the law in Durango."

"Or maybe just to get you."

Other bystanders were running up. "Boys, that was some shootin'," said one man, clearly a miner from his garb. "Never seen nothin' like it," another exclaimed. "Two at once, just like a shootin' gallery."

"Might have been a mite closer," a third interjected, "hadn't a been for that little gal with that there little pistol."

Charles Cavendish came running up. "Fast, boys that was fast, and accurate, and deadly. Caleb, do you know what a gem you have in this young man?"

"Reckon I do. By this time tomorrow, everyone in the whole territory will know too."

Cavendish turned to Luke, "Where's Laura?"

"In there." Luke indicated the mining office. "Charles would you mind walking her home? I've got a few things to do here. I'll be over just as soon as I get through. Please tell her that"

"I'd be happy to, Luke." Cavendish turned and walked into the mining office.

Chapter Thirteen

"Let's have a look at these jaspers," Caleb said.

Luke searched the pockets of the first man while Caleb looked through the pockets of the second man. The first man, Luke discovered, had $465 in gold coins. Caleb found $509 in gold and silver coins on the second man. Neither man had any sort of identification or other paper that might identify them.

"Well," Luke dryly observed, "It looks like the going rate for a Durango lawman is about five hundred dollars."

"Maybe more than that," Caleb said. Luke

looked over. "Unless I miss my guess, that five hundred dollars was just a down payment. The full amount was probably one thousand or maybe even more. No one was ever interested enough in me to pay that kind of money for me, dead. At least not on this side of the law." Caleb's eyes crinkled but he didn't smile. "You be careful, Luke. I've taken a real liking to you and I'd take it real personal if something happened to you."

"So would I, Caleb, so would I." *Especially now, with my having met Laura.*

When Caleb got back to his office there was no sound from the back. The gate to the cell was ajar and Red Barker had disappeared.

Caleb drew his pistol and ran outside. "Red's gone! Escaped!"

Luke came running up. "I'll look over this way and check the stable."

Caleb remarked to Luke later, "It appears that there was a nice little setup, to get all the attention on you and then free Red."

"I don't think Red is free. In fact, that cell would probably look good to him now. He should have talked when he had the chance." Caleb nodded his head.

"You know Caleb, if one of those two would have yelled 'Draw' and they'd both already had their guns in their hands, and then fired, they could have taken me easy. Why didn't they?"

"I think that's one time where your reputation helped you, Luke."

"How's that?"

"As sneaky as they were in the setup, if they'd shot you in the front, one of them could claim your scalp. Would have made them a real big man. Cutting you down after having the drop on you and yelling 'Draw' especially at a lawman, wouldn't help their reputations and could have gotten them hanged."

"I guess you're right about my reputation, Caleb. It cuts two ways."

"Yep."

The next few days were uneventful. The excitement of the gunfight had faded though not the local admiration of Luke's ability with a Colt. Consequently, when Caleb posted the "Carrying of Firearms Ban" there was very little grumbling, and rapid compliance.

With bad grace Varnes submitted to a search by Luke. Luke found nothing.

Chapter Fourteen

Replacing the excitement of the gunfight was the pending prizefight between Bob Cromwell and Jem Riley. The early betting was two to one on Cromwell. As the fight neared however, the odds shortened to three to two then almost even at six to five. On a hunch, Luke bet $100 on Riley. Since his bet was early, he got two to one odds. Eddie Roe took the bet and smiled. "You sure about that, Luke?"

Luke smiled back. "Nope, but I sure like the odds."

The day of the fight saw a brisk dawn that got colder as the day progressed. The sun shone as a

72

faint white orb giving little light and no heat. Clouds were forming in the north and the wind was starting to blow, bringing with it a portent of snow. For miles around the mines had closed down. The owners and foremen wanted to see the fight as much as the miners themselves. The cattlemen drew lots to see who would be in the skeleton crews to watch the herds. Anticipation was high and the bets ran hot.

The Lucky Dog was a beehive of activity. Roe was in his element, the stocky little man was everywhere at once—one time taking bets, then tending bar, then scrounging more lumber for makeshift bleachers. At five dollars a head for regular seating and $20 ringside, Roe couldn't afford to waste one square inch of space.

Into this holiday atmosphere stepped the two fighters. Cromwell was an imposing physical specimen. With his large upper body he towered over Riley who was still a large man. Cromwell wore dark blue boxing tights with a red and white sash tied around his middle. Riley sported black boxing tights with a green sash. His bald head gleamed from the overhead lanterns—it appeared to be coated with an oil or grease.

Both men wore high-top, lace-up, leather shoes. Cheers greeted both combatants as they stepped into the ring. As cold as it was outside, the inside of the Lucky Dog was warm with so many bodies packed closely together. The odors of tobacco, liquor, sweat and sawdust were magnified in the tight area.

The sheriff wore dark pants and his miner's boots but, especially for the occasion, he had donned a blue and white striped jersey as the referee. Caleb called the two men together in the middle of the ring. "Now boys," he said in a voice loud enough for the bleachers to hear, "London prize ring rules apply here, and I don't want any gouging or chawing or head-butting going on." The crowd let out a collective groan.

"And," Caleb continued, "I want only blows above the belt. When a man goes down that's the end of that round. The fight ends when a man is knocked out or can't continue. Or"—he looked pointedly at both fighters—"when I say it's over. All right, let's have a good fight."

A man at the side of the ring rang a bell and the fight commenced. Both fighters circled warily, their fists held up palms inward in the classic manner. Each fighter threw short stabbing left hands followed with a feint of the right, neither doing any damage. After about five minutes, Cromwell threw a tremendous right hand to the jaw of Riley. Riley went down and that ended the round.

The crowd broke into lusty cheers as Riley's handlers came and took him to his seat in the corner. Varnes came over to him, Riley looked up at Varnes and snarled something, then he looked over at Cromwell. Riley spit out a tooth on the edge of the ring, then he smiled. Riley's smile looked more villainous than his perpetual scowl.

Varnes was hurriedly placing as many more bets on Riley as he could, wheedling the best odds he could negotiate.

Since Luke was a deputy, and the only man legally armed, he was given a ringside seat. It was with some amusement that he observed Varnes betting as much as he could.

The bell sounded for the second round. Again, the fighters circled one another. Both fighters threw left hands feeling out each other. This time however, Riley pulled in his shoulders and arms to protect himself. Whenever Cromwell would throw a punch at his jaw, Riley would duck his head and take the punch on his thick forehead. The first time this happened Cromwell was shocked and surprised. He was not only not hurting Riley, he had also damaged his right hand on Riley's oily pate.

Riley countered with several combinations to the midsection then downed Cromwell with a left to the jaw to end round two. The crowd cheered lustily, the wagers were high, and the fight was living up to its expectations. Cromwell kept shaking and massaging his right hand as the bell for round three rang.

Riley's tactics were becoming obvious. Since all the bets had been laid down he had no need to make Cromwell look good. Riley would crouch and lead with his head while holding his shoulders in. Cromwell, who was punching now primarily with his left hand, could do no damage to Riley.

His blows had the same effect as if he had struck a cannonball. Occasionally Cromwell would get in a good punch and score a knockdown, otherwise it was all Riley, knocking Cromwell down, and ending the round.

In the twenty-third round Riley, using his head as a battering ram, raised up as if by accident and shattered Cromwell's nose. Blood flowed freely down his front, staining his pants and mixing with the sawdust. Another crashing right by Riley sent Cromwell down to end the round. Cromwell's handlers dragged him back to the corner to tend to his wounds. Along with his shattered nose, both of his eyes were swollen practically shut and his jaw was loose.

Caleb walked over to Cromwell's corner and looked at him. "How you doin', Bob?"

Cromwell peered up at him through threequarter-shut eyes. "I've felt better."

Riley looked from across the ring and sneered, "Watcha' gonna do Sheriff? Call the fight? I ain't even got goin' yet."

Caleb looked over at Riley. "If I call it Riley, I'll call it and you'll keep your mouth shut, understand?" Riley scowled.

Caleb said to Cromwell, "You've got nothing to prove Bob, you put up a game fight, Riley's a professional, that's all. He knows all the old tricks and a few new ones."

The bell rang. "One more round Caleb," Cromwell said.

"Good luck, Bob."

Chapter Fifteen

The twenty-fourth round went the same as the others except that Riley had Cromwell pinned against the ropes, his head was down and he was throwing lefts and rights at him. Cromwell's eyes were glazed, his arms were down at his sides, and he was making no attempt to defend himself. Caleb pulled Riley back.

Riley, mad with rage, turned, threw a short right hand and connected high on Caleb's cheekbone knocking him down. Caleb was stunned and temporarily unable to get up. The crowd was screaming and surging forward.

Luke put one hand on the ring post and vaulted

into the ring. He drew one of his single action Colts and, using the heavy barrel, soundly rapped Riley behind the ear. Riley's eyes rolled back in his head and he dropped down on both knees and then fell face forward into the sawdust.

At the same moment Cromwell went down on both knees and collapsed face forward also. Both combatants were out cold. The place was bedlam. People were screaming, hands were waving in the air. A few surged forward into the ring.

Luke took his Colt, the same one which had felled Riley, and fired into the ceiling. The gunshot reverberated in the packed house. The crowd quieted then fell silent.

Caleb got up shaking his head to get the cobwebs out. He looked at the two prostrate fighters and held up both his arms, the white and blue stripes of his jersey waved like flags in the smoky building. "I declare this fight a draw, all bets are off."

The decision was a popular one—a roar of approval erupted from the crowd. Most of the smart money had been put up by Varnes and a few others on Riley and the odds had been very favorable. Luke had taken his measure of the man and had made one of the few outside bets on Riley. The crowd laughed in merriment and cheers rang out all over.

Varnes came running up into the ring in an apoplectic rage, his face suffused with red. "You can't do that, Sheriff."

"'Pears like he already has, Varnes."

Varnes glared at Luke then back at Caleb. "But–but Riley was clearly the superior fighter of the two. He obviously won the fight."

"Oh, he won most of the rounds all right, I'll give you that," Caleb answered. "But you heard the rules, till one man can't continue. You see either one of them able to continue?"

Varnes looked at the two still forms and groaned. "You have any idea how much this is costing me?"

"Yeah, I got an idea," Caleb replied. "Serves you right for bringing in a ringer. A ringer who forgot which way to punch."

Eddie Roe was very happy with the decision. Along with most of the others, he had bet a lot on Cromwell. Now, with all bets off, the customers would have all the more money to spend drinking at the Lucky Dog. Both fighters were hauled back to their respective corners by their handlers. Neither one of them could quite comprehend what had happened.

Cromwell was trying to get up to fight a twenty-fifth round when his handler told him of the decision. In spite of the pain he was feeling throughout his body, Cromwell collapsed back on his stool and laughed. "A draw? The fight was a draw? I never been whipped so bad in my life and it was a draw? Ho, ho! Oh, ouch! It hurts to laugh."

Riley's reaction was understandably different. "A draw? That deputy slugged me from behind. T'wern't no draw nohow! I'm going to be getting me some even. That coward cost me a lot of money."

It had indeed cost Riley a lot of money since he had been promised a share of the betting profits. Varnes was still beside himself with rage. He had lost thousands of dollars in the non-decision. He told Riley, "I don't care how you do it, I want you to beat that deputy up so bad his mama won't recognize him. He's too good with a gun, I've already had that tried. You've got to get him to fight with fists. I'll pay you five hundred dollars when the job's done."

"It'll be a real pleasure, I'd almost do it for nothin'. I can use the five hundred though. Business has been right poor."

Laura had wanted nothing to do with the prize-fight. She heard the account of the fight with some amusement, however. Luke and Laura had become very close while pursuing leads about her father, Lars Jensen, after the gunfight in Durango. The mining claim Lars had first written about, while good, was not the strike that Lars had described to Laura in his subsequent letters. Lars had contracted out on "shares" in his silver claim. He had met two fellow Swedes, Ole Hansen and Gus Johnson, both of whom he trusted. They were given twenty percent each in his silver claim and worked very hard getting out the ore. Since they were very closed-mouthed and private, they seldom went into Durango, and chose instead to hire one of the haulers to get their supplies. The claim was not easy to find. Luke had to locate the hauler who took the supplies out and persuade him to tell where the claim was.

Luke and Laura had ridden out to the claim a few days before the fight and spoken with Ole and Gus. Both were big blond thickset men and appeared to be related. They seemed nonplussed to meet Laura and were openly hostile to Luke. When they were finally convinced that Laura was who she said she was they relented a little. "I can say nothing," Ole said in a sing-song voice, "until I get word to Lars. I know he loves you but he will not be happy you are here. I made a bad mistake—

I took some gold from the other claim to John Varnes' smelter. Varnes knows other claim not filed, and he tried many times to find Lars but he had no luck. Lars thinks if he files the claim then Varnes will find it and kill him. He knows it's very rich."

"How can you get word to Lars?" Luke asked.

"Where is he?" Laura asked.

"We have a system," Gus said in a similar sing-song voice. "We have three different secret places where we leave supplies for Lars. He leaves some gold ore then picks up his supplies. To answer your question, we don't know exactly where he is."

"How do you know where to go?" Luke asked.

"We leave notes, we have a code in Swedish based on places in the old country," Gus said. "They wouldn't make any sense to anyone not from Sweden. Even a Swede would not be able to figure it out."

"You go ahead and get word to Lars," Luke said. "If we don't hear from you we'll be back."

On the return trip, Laura was very excited that her dad was alive and apparently doing well with a new claim. Ironically, Lars had established an account with Wells Fargo. Luke mentally kicked himself for not having checked that avenue earlier,

although he might have had to reveal his undercover status to do so.

*No, wait, as a deputy I have a perfect right to in-
quire about the status of a depositor. I have to get
used to carrying a badge.*

Chapter Sixteen

After they got back to Durango, Luke took Laura to the Wells Fargo office. A clerk was out front and a manager was sitting in the back. The clerk was a small man with Ben Franklin glasses perched on his nose. He looked up from his desk and asked, "May I help you?"

"Hi," Luke said. "This is Miss Laura Jensen. She'd like to check on her dad's account, Mr. Lars Jensen."

"Mr. Thompson could you help these people?"

Cecil Thompson came waddling up from behind his desk. He was only five and a half feet tall but weighed at least two hundred and fifty pounds.

Having heard the conversation he avoided the pre-
liminaries. "Well now, you see we can't divulge
that information even if you are as you say—his
daughter—you are not authorized to see the account." Thompson stood back, a self-satisfied smile
on his face.

Luke fixed him with a cold stare. "Well, Laura, it
looks like it might take an extra day to uncover your
information. Of course, by that time Mr. Thompson
here will no longer be with Wells Fargo."

Thompson's face turned a chalky white. "Why—
why would that be?"

"By the time I get through sending a wire to
Jerome Puddington and an identical one to Lloyd
Tevis I reckon they won't have any more need for
your services. This little fellow here will probably
do just fine for a while."

"You actually know Mr. Puddington and and Mr.
Tevis?" Thompson's voice was now a high squeak.

"I should smile. Now Mister, you've got about
fifteen seconds to get that information or your job
won't be worth spit."

Thompson retrieved the ledgers with an alacrity
surprising in a large man. "Here you go. You can
understand why I wouldn't open them up without
a real good reason. We have to keep these things
confidential, you understand."

Luke looked at him. "Perfectly." Luke's initial impression of Thompson hadn't changed. He'd met him when he first came to Durango to collect the rewards on the bandits, and hadn't divulged his relationship with Wells Fargo. He'd been in the office a few times since to make a deposit to his account while in reality he was checking out the office.

Laura smiled sweetly. "Why thank you, Mr. Thompson."

"You're most welcome, Miss Laura," he said, avoiding Luke's gaze.

The deposits corresponded to the times Ole and Gus said that they'd been in town. The amounts were staggering, totaling more than fifty thousand dollars. Luke understood why Varnes was trying to find Lars. Murder wouldn't trouble Varnes a bit on the way to finding that claim.

Luke went back to the sheriff's office to find Caleb. Charles Cavendish looked up and smiled as Luke walked in. "Hi, Luke, just having a cup of coffee with Caleb."

Luke smiled at the energetic Scot. "Hello, Charles, you two still talking about that fight?"

Caleb laughed. "It must have been divine intervention that made me make that ruling. Of course when I saw Riley stretched out like a drying cowhide I just couldn't resist, especially after he'd knocked me down."

Luke and Cavendish both chuckled. "I don't think I've ever seen anything like the expression on Varnes' face when he was trying to get you to change your ruling," Cavendish said. "Jem Riley sure got more than he bargained for. By the way is he still around town?"

"Yeah, he is. I don't know why, though. His sort usually hightails it when there's no easy pickin's."

"Say, listen," Luke said. "Charles, you've saved five hundred dollars and there's good news about Laura's dad." Luke then told Caleb and Cavendish as much as he knew about Lars Jensen.

"I've got some news for you too, Luke," Caleb said. "I was riding out south and spotted something off the road in the brush. I might never have noticed except for the red color."

"Red Barker?"

"Yep, dead as a doornail. Shot three times in the back."

"That's too bad. If we'd had him a while longer I think he would have told us everything he knew."

"That's probably what whoever shot him thought too," Cavendish concluded.

"Yeah, dang it," Luke said. "We're not much

closer now than we were to finding out about those stagecoach robberies."

Caleb looked at Luke with a glint in his eye. "Maybe that's because you almost wiped out their gang single-handledly." Caleb and Cavendish chuckled. Luke just smiled and shook his head.

Chapter Seventeen

A few days later, Luke walked into the Lucky Dog. Off to the side sat Varnes, Riley and two others playing a slow game of poker. As Luke walked by Riley spoke up. "There goes a badge with a coward pinned to it."

Luke looked over. "You looking to get another bump on the skull, Riley? It'd match the one you got. In fact, a set of them might look good on you.

"You know, with a big old bare cannonball like you're carrying on your shoulders a few more bumps might look good, break up the monotony of having to look at all that ugly old bare skin."

A few of the onlookers farther away from the table laughed. Some of the closer ones tried to stifle chuckles, fearing Riley's wrath. Riley glared at the people around him and looked back at Luke. "Yeah, yer real tough with them guns on."

"Yep."

"Let's see how tough you are with them off."

"Nope. You know Riley, if you want to talk about cowards, you're sitting with just about the biggest coward in the whole state. Why don't you prove what a man you are and go slap old Varnes there around a little. I guarantee he won't do anything, at least not to your face. But then maybe he's paying you to stick around. Why would that be? To start trouble?"

Riley's eyes widened at the accusation of starting trouble for payment. He paused a moment to collect his thoughts.

At the mention of slapping Varnes, the crowd laughed again. Some looked at Varnes with derision. Luke walked on by and bellied up to the bar.

Eddie Roe was tending bar and came over with a worried look on his face. "I don't like this Luke, that bunch has been here a few days now. This is the first time they've paid any attention to anybody. I think they're after your hide."

"That's likely. Tell you what Eddie, get me a

beer mug and a bottle of the cheapest rotgut you can find."

Roe blinked, twice then started off. Luke's thoughts drifted back to the Circle D and Sing Loo: *Remember Luke, anything can be weapon.*

A minute later he was back with a bottle. "You know Luke, I could take offense at the idea that I might actually serve cheap whiskey."

Luke smiled. "Every so often I have to test the merchandise. It falls within my duty as a deputy."

Chapter Eighteen

Laura had never been in the Lucky Dog. It wasn't just that 'nice girls' didn't frequent a place like that, she simply had no desire to go there. So it was with some surprise that Luke saw her come in walking rapidly toward him. She was in a state of high excitement. "Luke, I have some news."

Before she could get to Luke, Jem Riley reached out and grabbed Laura and pulled her to him. "Here now girl, why don't you sit with a real man instead of that slicked-down deputy."

Laura rared back with her handbag to hit Riley but he was quicker and grabbed it away from her, looked at it, snorted, and threw it to Varnes. "I heard about that handbag, you ain't going to need it, you got me to protect you, 'stead a that coward." Riley laughed.

Varnes started to go through the handbag. He pocketed the Remington double derringer and pulled out some papers. Since Laura had spurned his advances he felt no need to be circumspect or polite.

Luke started over to the table at the first sign of interference with Laura.

Riley had on a loud drummer's suit but had removed his jacket. His shoulders were massive inside the white linen shirt. With his gleaming head he made a fearsome spectacle. He grabbed Laura around the waist and held her in front of him as easily as he might hold a kitten. "Just hold 'er right there Deputy, you don't want the little lady to get hurt none and you ain't gonna shoot no unarmed man."

"Don't count on it, Riley." Luke hissed.

"Tell you what, Deputy. You put up them guns and we'll have us a good old fashioned fight. How's 'at sound?" Riley laughed and tightened his grip cruelly on Laura and caused her to gasp with pain.

"All right, Riley. You've got what you want, let her go."

"First the guns, sonny boy, first the guns."

"Suppose I give you one of mine, Riley. You hold it in your hand and I'll leave the other one in the holster."

"No, Luke," Laura said wincing with pain.

"No, Luke. Aw, ain't that sweet. Well, Luke better move or he's going to have two halves 'stead of one whole girl."

Luke willed himself to remain calm. He knew that this was what Riley had been hanging around town for, why Varnes was keeping him here.

He was as angry as he had ever been in his life. The threat to Laura went against every code. Anyone who would harm a woman was a candidate for the hangman. Varnes and his crew had clearly been waiting for a situation like this, knowing that there was no way Luke could back out. Also knowing that Luke had to act or be thought a coward. Luke's blood was starting to sing and he could feel the familiar roaring in his ears, a prelude to combat.

At the first sign of trouble, Roe had dispatched one of his employees out the back door to get Caleb. Roe's eyes were wide and he was pale as Luke unbuckled his gun rig and put it up on the bar. Calmly, Luke handed his gun rig to Roe then took the bottle of rotgut and filled his mug with it.

He turned around and looked at Riley while taking a small sip of the whiskey. "Well, let's open the ball."

Riley wasn't one to be rushed, he was enjoying the attention once again. "Gonna drink some courage, boy? You're gonna need it." He shoved Laura over to Varnes, who pushed her away to one of his men.

"Hold her right close," Varnes ordered.

The third man was clearly uncomfortable with the mistreatment of Laura and, murmuring apologies, placed her in a chair by him.

Riley walked toward Luke. "Ain't gonna be no London prize ring rules nonsense. Gonna be catch as catch can, sonny boy, no holds barred, anything goes. How's your pretty face gonna like that, Deputy?"

Riley had crouched over so that, although he was taller, he was actually standing shorter than Luke. His arms were held in, his head was down to take any swing from any direction that Luke might throw. He would catch that swing on his head and injure or break Luke's hand.

"By the time I get through with you, that little lady over there won't even recognize you. She'll be sayin' 'No, Luke' 'cause she can't stand the sight of you. Ha ha." Riley was thoroughly enjoying himself now. "Gonna pay you back for that lump on the head you give me boy and fer stickin' your nose in where it didn't belong. Gonna pay you back good."

Riley started forward in his crouch, taking short shuffle steps. His fists were held close just under his cheeks. He feinted a few times with his left hand, testing Luke's reflexes. He outweighed Luke by thirty solid pounds but his experience in bare-knuckle fighting was far more of a factor.

As Luke started to step away from the bar, he reached out with the mug as if to put it down. Suddenly he turned around and with a flick of the wrist threw the entire contents of the mug into Riley's face—and eyes. Luke flipped away the mug which was deftly caught by Roe.

Riley let out a gasp that ended up in a howl. He began digging his fists into his eyes oblivious of everything but the searing pain. Still blinded, Riley grabbed in the air trying to get a grip on Luke. Luke stepped a half-step to the side and then transferred all his weight to his left foot as he gave a tremendous sweep with his right foot into Riley's shin, then raked it down his leg and stomped on his instep with his boot heel.

Riley let out another howl of pain and rage and crouched over further to take his weight off his injured foot. Luke stepped another half-step to the side and clasped his hands together, making of them a double fist in the shape of a blunt axe. He swung with all his might at the base of Riley's skull. The smacking sound of Luke's double fist connecting with Riley's neck could be heard above the roaring, and by now cheering, crowd.

Riley collapsed to his knees, his fists were held ineffectually out in front of him. He was shaking his head, trying to clear it. Ignoring Riley's fists, Luke stepped in and grabbed Riley's chin with one hand and his ear with the other. He slammed Riley's head twice against the edge of the bar. It struck with dull thuds.

As Riley fell forward, Luke put both hands behind Riley's head and propelled it downward into the brass footrail much as a kid would bounce a rubber ball. Riley's forehead hit with a sickening deep bong and rebounded from the footrail, after making a large crease in it. Riley was out cold with one arm looped around the bent footrail, hugging it like it was an old friend. A spittoon spun wildly off to one side like a child's top in play. The crowd erupted in cheers.

"Boys, that was quick," one of the onlookers exclaimed. "When ol' Luke goes to put a hurtin' on a body, he sure 'nuff does it quick."

"He shoulda stuck with them there London rules, Jem shoulda," said another. "When old Jem said anything goes I don't think he was thinkin' about a face full of booze. Hee hee."

Chapter Nineteen

A shot rang out with a deep boom followed closely by a sharper crack with an immediate exclamation of, "Ow, ow, ow, my arm, my arm."

Caleb had come in through the back door just as Luke threw the liquor into Riley's face. He put his short-barreled shotgun on a table. If he fired the shotgun in this crowd he might wipe out half the room.

As the fight was coming to its swift end, Caleb worked his way around to within fifteen feet of Varnes' table. The fourth man of the poker quartet had no compunctions about following any order given to him. So when Varnes told him to shoot an unarmed Luke, that's what he tried to do. As the gambler was taking careful aim with a Colt pocket pistol he had concealed Caleb drew and fired. Caleb's shot hit the man in the arm, and the man's reflex action sent the shot into the ceiling.

In the melee following the shots, Varnes grabbed Laura and dragged her to the door. He didn't have near the strength of Riley however and couldn't keep his hold on her. Laura broke away then turned around and raked Varnes face with her fingernails, drawing blood. Varnes yelled, then fled out the door still carrying Laura's handbag.

Luke rushed over to Laura and threw his arms around her. Laura winced but turned her head so Luke couldn't see her face, then she buried her face in Luke's shoulder and put her arms around him.

Caleb, having retrieved his shotgun, walked up to the man he had shot. The man, who had tried to backshoot Luke, was now looking pathetic, holding his right arm in pain. Caleb took no pity on the would-be back–shooter, he whipped the shotgun around in a half circle and smashed the man in the head. The man fell over like a toppled oak. The blood was flowing from his wounded arm and now his head. There was an ever-widening puddle of blood on the barroom floor.

Caleb looked at the fallen man and dryly observed, "Maybe that'll take his mind off his arm." Caleb walked over to Luke and Laura.

"That was pretty good shootin' Caleb."

"Aw, not so good Luke."

"What do you mean? You got him right in the arm, with a handgun too."

"Well, I wasn't aiming for his arm, I was aiming for his chest. I wanted to kill him."

"The way you brained him with that shotgun, I think you might have." Along with many of the onlookers Luke chuckled. "You were aiming for his chest and hit his arm, if that doesn't beat all." Despite her harrowing experience, Laura turned around and joined Caleb and the others in laughter.

Chapter Twenty

Laura pulled back and looked at Luke, "Oh, Luke, the reason I came in here was that I got a note from Dad along with a map. Now John Varnes has it."

"Do you remember the particulars?"

"I–I think so, most of them."

"We'd better get going. No telling what Varnes might do. Caleb, do you want to put those two in jail?"

"Yeah, but I think I better come with you, Luke. A few of the other boys can carry those two over to the jail. Merv's a part-time deputy, he can watch them while we're gone. They won't be making any trouble for a while."

"What about him?" Luke asked indicating the profusely bleeding fourth man, whose name was Baldwin.

"The bullet went through him. They can get Clancy, the barber, to come over and bind him up. Either he'll live, or he won't, I don't much care which."

The third gambler, named Stockard, stood up. He was pale from what had happened to the other gambler, and Riley. "I don't hold with mistreating womenfolk," he said while he looked back and forth between Luke and Caleb. His glance dropped to the floor when he looked at Laura. "I'm right sorry about all this, but I am through with that bunch."

Caleb gave him a hard, unforgiving look. "That's fine, as far as it goes. We want to know what you know about Varnes and his plans."

"I don't know much," Stockard said. "Varnes kept everything pretty much to himself. I do know that he was going to pay Jem Riley to beat up Luke Dawson real bad. I also know he won't go out of town without Homer Biggs and a few others riding along with him."

"I've seen Biggs around, he's the foreman over at the smelter," Luke said.

"Yeah, he does some other jobs for Varnes too but I'm not sure what all," Caleb added.

"All I can tell you," Stockard said, "is that for being the foreman he's gone a lot. The day that Luke killed those two gunfighters, Biggs wasn't at the smelter."

"That might explain about Red," Luke said.

"Yeah, and a few other things," Caleb said. "We'd better get going."

"I'm coming too," Laura said.

Luke and Caleb both looked at her. "It could be bad, Laura. It's likely there will be shooting."

"Luke's right, Laura," Caleb said.

"You think I can't hold up my end?" she asked with a challenge in her voice.

"That's not it," Luke said softly.

"I don't care. It's my dad, I have to know." Caleb and Luke looked at each other, lips pursed, and mutually shrugged in resignation.

"We'd better get at least two more men to go with us," Caleb said.

Eddie Roe, who had served as a part-time deputy before, piped up from behind the bar, indicating another bartender. "Dave and I can go, I wouldn't want to miss the excitement. I'll even bring along some whiskey, for medicinal purposes you understand, a lot better brand than Luke uses too." Everyone chuckled.

"All right." Caleb raised his voice. "You men,"

indicating some on-lookers he knew, "carry these two over to the jail. Then go get Clancy to treat that one's wounds." Caleb looked at Stockard. "I'm letting you go, though I could, and probably should, jail you with the others."

"I appreciate that, Sheriff. Is it okay if I stay around town for a while?"

"Just stay out of trouble."

Stockard nodded.

Snow had fallen intermittently for the previous two days, and was starting to fall again as the group went out to get its horses. The wind was coming out of the north, swirling the snow in flurries as it swept into Durango.

Caleb looked over at Eddie. "Would you go down to the smelter and see if Varnes is still there? He may not want to go out in this weather."

"I'll check on him." Roe took off at a run.

Luke looked at Caleb. "We'd better get some sheepskin coats, buffalo robes, groundsheets and some other supplies if we're going out in this."

"Are you absolutely sure you want to go, Laura?" Caleb asked.

"Yes, I have to see my dad. I have to know he's all right," Laura answered emphatically.

Roe came back from the smelter. "It looks like Varnes and some others have left. There are two armed guards out front so I couldn't get too close. I did see a group of horsemen riding out and circling around to go north."

"Let's hurry and stock up," Caleb said. "We've got to try to catch them."

Their supplies were picked up in short order, mostly dry food like jerked beef, dried apricots, coffee, bread and beans. They also stocked up on ammunition, most of it .44-40s for the Winchesters and Colt pistols. Luke added three boxes of the long .50 Sharps cartridges.

He put his Winchester on the packhorse and strapped the Sharps, the trophy from the Bar H fight, onto his big dun. The fringes of the buckskin scabbard danced merrily as the dun pranced around, smelling excitement, anxious to get going.

Laura refused any help in packing and had also included a Winchester in her repertoire. She had, however, allowed Luke to provide her with a set of Remington over and under derringers. "Thank you, Luke, I've grown accustomed to the feel of those little guns."

In spite of the danger of the situation, Luke chuckled. "I'm afraid I've got me a real spitfire."

"Luke," Laura answered smiling, "you don't know the half of it."

All of the group was wearing oversized sheepskin

coats. Scarves held down their hats and were also wrapped around their necks. The big soft collars were turned up to ward off the snow. Warmth, and therefore survival, was the order of the day, not fashion.

Luke addressed the group, "I think we'd better check out the silver claim first. It's in the general direction of the gold claim anyway, isn't it, Laura?" Laura nodded.

With Luke in the lead, the group galloped out of town, following the hoofprints in the newly fallen snow wherever possible. The wind and increasing snowfall made it difficult at times to spot just what direction Varnes' bunch had taken and how many of them there were. Caleb followed Luke, with Laura riding third. Roe trailed the packhorse behind him and Dave brought up the rear. Dave had been with Roe for two years and was a quiet and dependable young man. Roe knew that Dave would be a strong support in a fight. They'd been there together before.

Chapter Twenty-one

Within two miles of town the countryside turned mountainous. The route was a little different from the one Luke and Laura had taken originally but was still headed in the general direction of Lars Jensen's silver claim. The group, still looking for hoofprints, was riding single file up a trail.

On either side of the trail were outcroppings of rocks extending far up the sides of the mountains. The snowstorm had abated somewhat but the sky was still a late afternoon dark and the temperature was bitterly cold. Just ahead and far up in the rocks a sound pealed forth like the opening crash of a thunderstorm.

Luke glanced up and saw just a wisp of smoke as it was taken away by the wind. Dave let out a sigh as he toppled off his horse in a kind of slow motion. There was a group of boulders off to the side of the trail about 30 yards away.

Luke yelled and swatted his horse while pointing the way. "Over here, over here." He whirled around past Caleb and rode alongside Laura, shielding her with his body.

They arrived at the boulders at about the same time. Luke, Caleb and Laura dismounted. Roe dropped the rope of the packhorse and rode back out to check on Dave. He rode fast and low keeping to the far side of his horse. The deep booms continued—bullets landed with a thud into the ground or ricocheted off the rocks with a fading whine.

Dave's panic-stricken horse galloped back down the trail as Roe approached. It took only a glance for him to see that Dave was dead. The first shot had hit him high in the chest, others had taken off part of his head. Roe turned his horse and galloped back toward the boulders, again staying on the far side of his horse by hunkering down with his foot in one stirrup.

Ten yards short of the boulders a shot killed Roe's horse. It cartwheeled and flung him clear.

Roe managed to grab his Winchester from the saddle scabbard and dart back to the boulders.

Puffing and coughing, his eyes red, Eddie said, "Dave's dead. He never even knew what hit him."

Caleb warily looked up over the edge of a boulder and a bullet pinged off the big rock in greeting. "They set this up real pretty," he said. "We can't ride forward, we'd be too long exposed. We can't ride back they'd have a perfect shot. They waited until we got right here and shot the last man in line, knowing we'd come for these rocks. Now we're pinned down like a butterfly on a board."

"What do you think they're shooting?" Luke asked.

"Probably government Springfields, .45-70s most likely, or they might have some Sharps."

"They're pretty far up. I can see the smoke about five seconds before I hear the sound."

"A little better than half a mile away," Caleb calculated.

"That's way out of the range of these Winchesters," Roe said.

"I'm sure they figured on that," Luke replied.

"I wish I'd stayed behind, Luke," Laura said. "If I weren't here you could probably make it out."

"We'd probably be dumb enough to try. That's

112   *Denny Andrews*

just what they want. Let's make them real confident."

"How can they be any more confident than they already are?" Caleb asked.

"Lets get out the Winchesters." Then Luke explained his plan.

Chapter Twenty-two

Caleb, Laura and Roe unlimbered their .44-40-caliber Winchester Model 73 rifles. They put them up over the rocks and got down behind them as far as they could. Then they proceeded to fire in the direction of the entrenched bushwhackers.

The Winchesters made sharp cracking noises compared to the deep boom of the bushwhackers' Springfields. As expected, the Winchesters' bullets fell far short of the bushwhackers. With their being so far up the canyon wall there was no way for .44-40 bullets to make it.

Their efforts were met with derisive laughter from the bushwhackers. One of the men stood up, and to get a better angle at the group was firing from the off-hand position, his bullets coming in uncomfortably close.

Another man also stood up but he was turned around with his back to them, slightly bent over, mockingly patting his backside, a universal gesture of contempt.

Temporarily out of view, Luke ducked down and went to the far side of his horse. He tried to soothe the big dun with a few soft words.

Luke knew he would have less than five seconds to get off two aimed shots. Once they heard the big boom of his Sharps the bushwhackers wouldn't so much as peek over the rocks again. *I've got one chance. And a slim one at that. Lord let me shoot straight.*

Luke took the big single-shot Sharps from the scabbard and loaded it. In his other hand, between his fingers, he carried three of the long .50-caliber cartridges. He sat down with his back against the boulders as he put the Sharps up to his shoulder, still out of sight of the bushwhackers. Flipping up the long-range Vernier peep sight on the buttstock of the weapon, he looked through it and got a steady focus.

The wind had died down somewhat but there

was still a high-pitched moan as it flowed from the north and caressed the canyon. Luke's heart was beating fast and he was taking deep breaths. Saying another quick prayer, Luke stood up and whirled, setting his elbow on the top of a rock all in one instant.

He drew a bead on the man who was firing at them, aiming slightly above his head to allow for the drop of the bullet. Barely touching the trigger, the Sharps exploded against his shoulder with a roar. The one-ounce bullet went on a true path taking out the stomach and the back of the first bushwhacker.

Luke didn't have time to admire his handiwork. Jerking the trigger guard down, he hurriedly ejected the spent shell and inserted another. He cocked the hammer of the Sharps and pulled the first trigger all in one motion. Taking a deep breath, he held it then slowly exhaled. This was possibly the only chance they would have to get out. If anyone else came back from the main bunch, they would be pinned down in a crossfire and be slowly picked apart.

Only the arrogance of the second bushwhacker saved the small group at the boulders. He was still standing patting himself when he heard the clatter of his partner's Springfield in the rocks. By the time he turned his head and heard the subsequent roar of Luke's big Sharps it was too late. Luke's second bullet caught him just below the shoulder blades and propelled him face down into the rocks.

The echoes of Luke's Sharps reverberated in the canyon, then finally a stillness settled in, punctuated by the ever present freezing wind.

The group looked at one another. Laura was the first to speak. "Oh, Eddie, I'm so sorry about Dave. I know you two were close." Roe merely nodded, he found himself unable to speak.

"Darn shame," Caleb said. "But boy Luke, that was sure some shootin'. You suckered them out of their hideyhole real good. I'd say they were right surprised."

"Thanks," Luke said. "It was a little luck and a lot of help from the Lord. Caleb, you see to Dave and I'll go up in the rocks and see how those boys were set up."

"All right. You watch out, Luke. Keep your eyes peeled." Luke nodded.

Caleb, Roe and Laura moved Dave off the trail and put rocks over his body to keep predators away. Meanwhile, Luke left his rifle and started his long trek up into the rocks. It wasn't a particularly steep climb but it was tiring.

When he got there he was somewhat surprised. This wasn't just a place of opportunity, it was a well set up ambush site. There was a small cave to the rear where the bushwhackers were planning to have a fire. Both men had been dressed warmly and apparently were ready for a long wait.

They were sent out to wait for us. It wasn't if, it was just a matter of when. Their wait will now be much longer.

He thought he recognized the two men from the crowd at the Cromwell-Riley fight but wasn't positive. Gathering up the rifles, ammunition and food, he wrapped the supplies in two buffalo robes, lashed them together, and started back down.

They had redistributed the weight of the supplies among the horses. Roe took the saddle off of his dead horse and put it on the packhorse. The group pushed on but within an hour it was apparent they weren't going to make any more progress that day. The fight had slowed them considerably and it was almost dark. They went up into a stand of pines and made camp.

First, they cut boughs for shelter and tied them together. Then they built a small fire at the entrance of the shelter. Using the extra buffalo robes, along with their own, they hunkered down for the night. Snow was falling again and it was bitterly cold. They kept the fire going throughout the night.

Chapter Twenty-three

Dawn revealed that an additional foot of snow had fallen. That combined with the snow already on the ground would make the going tough. The foursome had a quick breakfast of coffee, biscuits and bacon. After packing up, they started off for Lars' silver claim.

Driven by the wind, the snow was coming at them parallel to the ground. A few miles farther on, they came upon the silver claim. There was no sound of the steady clink of the pickax or the crunch of the shovel that Luke and Laura had heard on their previous arrival.

"That's strange," Laura said. "I didn't think

anything like a little old blizzard would stop Ole and Gus from working."

"I don't like it," Luke answered. "There should be some kind of activity."

Caleb interrupted the observations. "Eddie, you stay here with Laura, Luke and I'll go down to see what's going on." Laura and Roe both nodded.

Luke and Caleb took out their Winchesters and carried them across their saddlebows as they rode into the claim. The only sound was the wind. Otherwise there was utter silence.

Luke was the first to spot the misshapen mound in the snow. It was adjacent to a rock, almost, but not quite blending in. Luke rode over and dismounted, trailing the reins behind him. He brushed the snow away from the mound and stared into the sightless eyes of Gus Johnson.

"Caleb, over here," Luke called in a conversational tone. He didn't want to alarm Laura and Roe.

Caleb rode over and dismounted. He looked at Gus then gently rolled him over. There were three bullet holes in his back. "Any one of those shots would have killed him, Luke."

"Looks like they wanted to make sure."

Off to the side was a tiny mining shack. Luke and Caleb rode over to it, fearing the worst. It was not unexpected therefore when they came upon Ole Hansen in the shack dead. He apparently had undergone some brutal questioning before being murdered because his face had been beaten and severely bruised.

"How long do you think they've been dead, Caleb?"

"Gus, maybe six to eight hours, Ole maybe two."

"We should have pushed on last night."

"You know better than that, Luke. In that snowstorm we'd probably have gotten lost if we hadn't froze to death. If it had been just you and me trying to get here we wouldn't have done any better. Now, we just have to get going, see if we can save Laura's dad."

Luke and Caleb rode back and explained what they had found to a shaken Roe and Laura. "Where did the map say to go from here, Laura?" Caleb asked.

"It started from here and extended north further into the San Juans," Laura answered. "Then it extended west through the mountains to the base of the Needles."

"About ten miles total," Caleb said.

"I wasn't sure of the distance. I was sure that Dad wanted Ole and Gus to accompany me and anyone else I brought along. I think they really knew where Dad's gold claim is located. The map wasn't very clear, unless you know Swedish."

"That explains about their torturing Ole. Let's get going," Caleb said.

"What about Gus and Ole?" Roe asked.

"We'll put Gus in the shack," Luke answered. "That's the best we can do for now. Anything else would take too much time. We have to try to save Lars if we can."

Chapter Twenty-four

The four pressed on as fast as they could go. They ate in their saddles, a meal of cold biscuit and jerked beef with water to wash it down. By the afternoon they had passed the spot in the San Juans and were moving on toward the Needles. Up ahead they heard a series of pops and crashes, which sounded like ice breaking off the rocks up above.

"What's that?" Laura asked with dread.

"Gunshots," Caleb answered grimly. "Let's go!"

"Wait!" Luke yelled. "Let's unlimber those

Springfields and my Sharps and fire a few rounds. We'll let Lars know that help is on the way and give those scum something to think about."

Caleb, seeing the wisdom of Luke's suggestion, was already jerking a Springfield out of his pack. Roe was grabbing the other one and Luke had his Sharps out. They all began firing toward the gun-fire sounds as they were riding in. Laura fired her Winchester in the air, adding to the cacophony. Ten minutes later they pulled into the base of the Needles.

The snow had stopped but the wind was still strong and gusting. John Varnes, Homer Biggs and three others had pulled out and were riding for all they were worth, half a mile away.

Luke was off his horse before it stopped. He hurried over to a rock and rested his elbow on it. Controlling his breathing, he took a moment to aim. He cocked the hammer and pulled the first trigger. Taking careful aim through the peep sight, the Sharps exploded against his shoulder with a roar and a mighty kick.

One of the riders in the back of the bunch stiff-ened in his saddle, then he lurched forward trying to hang on to the saddle horn. His horse kept gal-loping but it appeared that the man was suddenly riding a bucking bronco. There was no rhythm between horse and rider. The man let go and toppled into the snow. His horse kept going a short distance then stopped. The rest of the bunch kept riding, no one looked back.

Luke loaded a fresh cartridge into his Sharps. He shot just as the bunch was rounding a far bend, disappearing from sight. If his second shot had any effect he couldn't tell. Off to the side, and partially camouflaged in a copse of trees, there was a small miner's cabin. There were many bullet holes in the front and the sides.

Fearing the worst, the four ran to the cabin and tore open the barricaded door. On the floor propped against the mattress lay a man, unconscious and barely breathing.

Lars Jensen.

He had three visible bullet wounds but there might have been more. The blood was slowly ebbing from him.

In front of him he had laid out a Winchester, a shotgun and a Remington new model Army revolver converted to cartridge. There were over one hundred empty shells scattered around and several open boxes of ammunition. Clearly, Lars had given a good account of himself.

Laura was the first to reach Lars. "Dad, oh Dad, Dad, can you hear me?"

Lars' eyelids fluttered. "Wha? Laura? How? Where am I?" Then he lapsed back into unconsciousness.

"Laura," Caleb said gently. Laura looked at him. "Don't try to revive him again. We'd better take a look and see if we have to do any cutting on him or if the bullets all went through. It would be better to do it while he's asleep."

Tears streaming down her face, Laura only nodded in reply.

"It's cold in here, really cold, almost as bad as outside," Luke said. "I'll go unload the buffalo robes. You might want to put that mattress upright on the bed so we can make him as comfortable as possible."

Roe went out with Luke to help unload some supplies. True to his word, Roe had brought some bottles of good Kentucky bourbon. "I think these will come in handy. Lars is sure going to need some and maybe we will too."

In spite of himself, Luke chuckled. "Darn if I know why I'm laughing, Eddie but you're probably right. I could probably use a jolt of that stuff myself—maybe after things get settled down."

They got Lars into bed and inspected his wounds. One bullet had gone through his side, another had grazed his skull, and the third was still lodged in his shoulder. There were no other wounds.

"We've got to get that out," Caleb said. "Otherwise infection will set in and he'll die. I've seen it before."

"Let's get a fire goin'," Roe said. "Boys, it's cold in here."

"Good thing," Caleb remarked.

"Why's that?" Luke asked.

Caleb replied: "If it hadn't been as cold as it is in here he'd have bled to death from that side wound alone. The cold slowed the flow of the blood."

"I didn't even think of that but you're right Caleb. I'm going to go and retrieve that horse, we can use it. Then, if you'll get the fire going I'm going to look for some plants and roots."

"Whatever for?" Eddie asked.

"For some remedies to treat the wounds and maybe for him to drink along with that who-hit-john. A friend showed me a lot of concoctions and poultices to make just from plants."

"Indian?" Caleb asked.

"No, although they probably use a lot of the

same things. This fellow is Chinese, Sing Loo, as close to a brother as I ever had."

Laura turned from her father and looked up at Luke in wonderment. There was so much about him she didn't know, and so much more she wanted to know. "Whatever you think will help, Luke, please do it."

Luke nodded and went back out into the bitter cold. He grubbed around for half an hour picking up pine needles and various other plants. He dug down through the snow with his big Bowie knife and pulled out some roots that he recognized.

When he gathered what he thought was enough he went back inside the shack. A fire was going in the small stove, one pan was on it, water boiling. Luke set to work.

They carefully cleansed and bound the two wounds where the bullets had exited. The third they surveyed. "Have either of you done this before?" Luke asked.

Roe shook his head, a queasy expression on his face.

"Some," Caleb answered.

"Good," Luke said, relieved. "'Cause I haven't, and I sure don't want to start learning now."

In a very low voice, out of Laura's hearing, Caleb replied, "Don't get to feeling too good. I haven't had the best luck doin' this, that's why I'm a sheriff, not a doctor."

"Do the best you can, Caleb," Luke said in an equally low voice. "I'm sure your worst will still be better than my best."

Chapter Twenty-five

Luke went to work boiling the roots and plants he had found. When he had everything prepared, he nodded to Caleb to begin.

"I want you boys to hold him," Caleb said. "When I start in, he may commence to kick some and thrash around."

With Luke on one side, Roe on the other and Laura holding his legs, Caleb started to operate. Lars did thrash around but in his weakened condition couldn't put up much of a fight. Finally, using a knife and a bent straight fork, Caleb extracted the bullet from Lars' shoulder.

"Looks like a .44 caliber," Luke said.

"Yep. Probably came through the wall first and slowed some before it hit his shoulder. That's why it didn't go all the way through him."

"What happens now?" Laura softly asked.

All three men looked at her. Luke was the first to speak. "Well, now we just wait for a few days until he's ready to travel. Then we rig up a travois and we all head to Durango."

"What's a travois?" Laura inquired.

"It's an Indian rig. Basically it's a long stretcher dragged by a horse. It'll be easier on your dad than if he tried to ride."

Caleb and Roe nodded in assent. Left unsaid was the possibility, in fact the probability that Lars wouldn't recover. While Caleb and Roe gathered wood in preparation for another storm, Luke went hunting for food with his Winchester.

He shot a big buck, which became too curious, about a mile from the shack. Hurrying back to the shack, he quickly retrieved his horse and rode back to collect his kill. A few shots scattered the hungry wolves that were already gathering. Using his Bowie knife, Luke dressed the buck on the spot. The wolves would get a share after all. Venison stew was the meal of the day and for days after that for the small group.

After a day, Lars gradually regained consciousness. Later on, when he took a drink of watered whiskey and a little broth, everyone breathed a sigh of relief. It appeared that he was on the mend. The mending was slow however and for the most part he slept. The poultices that Luke made didn't seem to hurt. In fact, they seemed to help. A few days later, Lars was finally sitting up taking more nourishment.

Caleb asked him about the events leading up to the gunfight.

"I saw that bunch riding up this way and immediately got suspicious. They were trying to appear too casual even though it was clear this was their destination. Also, there were too many of them for this to be a friendly visit. I laid out my weapons and put up what barricade I could and waited."

"What did they say they wanted?" Luke asked.

"We didn't have much conversation on that point. They just said they knew I had some gold hidden. They wanted it and then they'd let me go free. Somehow, I didn't believe them. I fired a few shots, and then went back inside and blocked the door. It was a pretty good fight 'til I got hit."

"Too bad Ole and Gus weren't a little more suspicious," Roe added.

"What about Ole and Gus?" Lars asked.

Laura recounted the events that led them to

rescue Lars. When she came to the part about Ole and Gus, Lars closed his eyes and slowly shook his head. "I knew we should never have sent that one gold shipment to Varnes' smelter. Now my two friends are dead."

"I think Varnes intends to file on this claim," Luke said. "Now that he knows where it is, the sooner we can get you back to Durango, to file yourself, the better."

Within a day, Lars said he was ready to travel. Laura knew he was still too weak but she also knew her dad couldn't be dissuaded. As Luke had mentioned, they rigged a travois. They cut the trailing edges long so they would operate like a sled going through the snow. With the piling up of buffalo robes above and below him, Lars' comfort was better than might have been expected.

The trip back to Durango took two full days. With frequent changing of dressings and the consumption of warm broth, Lars' condition, while it didn't improve, didn't worsen either. Caleb and Luke alternated riding point and drag. They kept a vigilant eye on any potential ambush spots.

The town was quiet when the group rode in. They headed straight over to the Lincoln boardinghouse and got Lars settled. Mrs. Cray fussed and clucked and insisted that he take her room on the ground floor. "It's more spacious," she said, "and much more comfortable."

Roe stopped off at the Lucky Dog and Caleb rode over to the sheriff's office to check on his prisoners. Roe rode back from the saloon with Merv in tow about the same time that Caleb came boiling out the door of the jail.

"What happened?" Caleb yelled.

Merv spoke up. "When Varnes and Biggs and the other two rode back in they came in with drawn guns and freed Riley and Baldwin. Baldwin's still in pretty sorry shape, even though Clancy patched him up. They had to carry him. They almost left him here. Riley was recovered and madder'n a wet hen."

"Where'd they go?" Caleb asked.

Roe chimed in. "First they went to the mining office, then they made a quick stop at Wells Fargo. As far as we know, they all went over to Varnes' smelter."

"Let's go over to the Lincoln and talk to Luke," Caleb said. "We'll sort this out."

They all rode over to the Lincoln, dismounted, stomped the snow off their boots, and went into the front room. Luke joined them. Mrs. Cray brought them hot coffee, which was gratefully accepted.

After Roe and Merv got through telling Luke

what had happened, Luke sat there for a few moments. "Caleb, would you go over to the mining office and I'll check with Wells Fargo. We'll see what they've been up to before we move on them."

Laura walked in and the four stood up. "C'mon, you three should know me well enough not to stand on ceremony." She laughed. They smiled and sat down.

"How's Lars?" Caleb asked.

"I think Mrs. Cray has made him feel at home. He's resting now. That trip took some out of him."

They told Laura what was going on and warned her to be on the lookout for any trouble from Varnes or any of his hirelings.

"All right," Luke said. "I'll go on over to Wells Fargo, Caleb will go to the mining office. Eddie, can the Lucky Dog do without you for a little while longer?"

"You bet it can." The compact little man was bristling with righteous anger still over the senseless death of Dave, his friend. "I'm ready to finish this, what do you want me to do?"

"I'd appreciate it if you'd stay here with Laura for now, in case Varnes has any bright ideas."

"I'll do it. Merv, go back to the Lucky Dog and get two more of the boys to come and help stand guard."

"Who?" Merv asked.

"Maybe Rogash and Louis," Roe answered. "No, instead of Louis get Zeb. Have Louis mind the saloon."

Luke turned and looked at Roe at the mention of the last name, "Zeb? Short for Zebulon?"

"I suppose. I don't think you've met him yet Luke. He just drifted in a month ago. He's done a few odd jobs for me and done 'em well. He seems salty enough, why"

"Probably nothing. I suppose there are a lot of folks named after old Zebulon Pike or Zebulon right out of the Old Testament. Let's meet back here in an hour, okay?"

Caleb nodded and he and Luke went out the door together. Laura sat down and began altering the pockets on a warm wool dress, by lining them with leather. Roe thought it was a curious thing to do, but said nothing.

Chapter Twenty-six

The snow had continued falling in Durango and was a good three feet deep in most places. In other areas it had drifted and was much deeper.

When Luke walked into the Wells Fargo office the skinny clerk was still out front and Cecil Thompson was sitting in the back. The clerk looked up from his work, his eyebrows raised, and there was a curious expression on his face. When Thompson saw Luke walk in, his eyes narrowed. Clearly there was no love lost between them. He didn't get up. "What can I do for you?" he asked brusquely.

"I want to know every piece of business John

Varnes has with Wells Fargo and with you." A sus-
picion was forming in Luke's mind but remained
unsaid.

At the reference to himself, Thompson turned
red, then crimson. "I've known Mr. Varnes for some
time now, and I'm not going to discuss his business
with nothing more than a local deputy, or the sheriff
either for that matter. I allowed that questioning the
last time you were here to slide, in deference to
Miss Jensen, but this time it's different."

"How different?" Luke was suddenly enjoying
himself.

"Well, I made inquiries at headquarters and no
one knew you."

"All right let's do away with this sideshow."
Luke reached down into his boot in a concealed
interior pocket and pulled out his Wells Fargo
Special Agent badge. "You know what this is?"

Thompson stared at the badge, nonplussed.

"Get up and come over here you jumped up bag
of hog swill!"

The curious skinny clerk suddenly got very un-
curious. He buried his face in the ledger he was
working on. Thompson started to reach into his
desk drawer, saw the look on Luke's face, and
thought better of it. The transformation in Thompson's countenance was a wonder to behold. He

went from red-faced anger to a blanched expression, white as a sheet.

"I–I–I'm sorry, er Deputy, er Luke, er Special Agent Mr. Dawson. I had no idea who you were. But–but no one told me any anything."

"You weren't supposed to, and they weren't supposed to. Now, if you want to keep your job, tell me what I want to know, everything."

"Well Mr. Varnes came in and said he'd filed on a claim out north by Bald Butte and that any gold that was taken out of there by Lars Jensen rightly belonged to him. Since Lars had met an unfortunate accident, he didn't want to make trouble for his daughter. He just wanted all the money in the Wells Fargo account, since it was rightfully his."

"How kind of him. What did you tell him?" Luke softly asked.

"I–I said I'd look into it and let him know in a few days."

"That's it?" Luke asked with an intense expression on his face. Thompson nodded, his jowls jiggling like jelly just out of the tin.

Luke looked at the clerk who was still buried in his ledger. "What do you say, skinny?" The clerk looked up. "Your job depends on whether I get the truth, not on what Thompson says is the truth."

The clerk looked at Luke, back at Thompson

and back again at Luke. "Well, Deputy, Mr. Dawson, Cecil did say that he'd go ahead and transfer the money right after there weren't nobody to object to it."

"That's it," Luke said. "Thompson you're fired. I really do wish you'd reach back into that drawer."

Thompson said nothing, he was getting paler by the second. He kept his hands flat on the desk top. He looked at his now former clerk with pure venom. The clerk, to Luke's surprise, returned the look, without flinching.

"I'll just collect my things," Thompson said with as much dignity as he could muster.

"You'll collect nothing," Luke replied. "In fact, empty your pockets. I want to see exactly what you have on you."

"But you can't—"

"I can do anything I want. If you want to jaw any longer, I'll make you strip and run you out in the snow."

The skinny clerk put his head back deep into the ledger to keep his smile hidden. Apparently, Cecil Thompson hadn't been the kindest of bosses. With the discussion obviously at an end, Thompson emptied his pockets onto the desk. Luke went over and looked through the pile. He pulled out all the paper and the set of keys to the front door. The money, watch and penknife he gave back to Thompson.

"Headquarters shall hear of this," Thompson sniffed.

"They sure 'nuff will. I'm going to be doing some checking on you Thompson. In the meantime, I wouldn't try for another job at Wells Fargo or any other express company for that matter. Now get out."

Thompson exited the office, slamming the door. They could hear his boots crunching in the deep snow and the sound faded into the distance.

Luke looked at the clerk. "Well, skinny, your first duty is to go over to the hardware store and get several hasps and locks—seven should do it. Then I want you to install two on the front door and the rest as you see fit. Also, get two sets of keys."

"Yes sir, Mr. Dawson?"

"Call me Luke."

"Okay, sir, Mr. Dawson, er Luke."

Luke raised his eyebrows.

The skinny clerk rushed on. "My name is Sam, Sam Ball."

"Is that for Samuel?"

"No sir, for Samson, I think my dad had a sense of humor." Ball was small, about five-foot-five and about one hundred and twenty-five pounds. His hair was a dark brown and his eyes a penetrating blue.

Luke smiled, his eyes crinkled at the corners. Suddenly he felt older than his years. He regretted referring to the clerk as skinny. The events of the previous few days had taken their toll.

"It's a good name," Luke softly replied. "Right out of the heart of the Old Testament. I think your dad named you well."

Ball sat up straight and looked directly at Luke. He felt he could work for this man. He suddenly felt better than he had felt at this job in a long time. "I'll get right on those hasps and locks, Luke."

"Good, and, oh Sam?" Ball looked at Luke as he was shrugging into his sheepskin coat. "You're now the station manager. You've got a raise coming. Do the job, and I'll see you're well taken care of." Ball felt a tingling as he hurried over to the hardware store. He didn't think it was only the cold that made him feel that way.

Chapter Twenty-seven

Sam Ball came back from the hardware store
and started in to work on the front door to install
the new locks. Luke went to Thompson's desk and
pulled out the Colt single action revolver. On the
backstrap it said PROPERTY OF W F & CO.

Luke held the pistol crossways in front of him.
"Hey, Sam." Ball stopped working and looked up.
"You know how to handle one of these things?"

Ball nodded. "Not like you do, not even close.
I've seen you practice and in action. I did serve a
hitch with General Crook, up on the Platte, back
in '75 though."

Luke smiled and nodded. You just never knew

about a person. He chided himself for having had the wrong first impression of Ball. "Good, I don't have to tell you there may be trouble from old Cecil. I'm not worried about him, but that crowd he runs with is ruthless. So be ready. When you get through there would you check everything in the office as well as the ledgers?"

"Sure thing." Ball replied and went back to work.

Luke left the Wells Fargo office and made a stop at the telegraph office. He sent a quick wire to Jerome Puddington about his action in firing Thompson and asked for a rapid return wire confirming Sam Ball's appointment as station manager and subsequent raise in pay. He also asked for the dates and locations of the stage robberies and whether Thompson could have known of any valuable shipments on them. Then Luke hurried back to the Lincoln to see Caleb and Roe—and Laura. He brightened up when he walked in and saw them sitting there.

"What happened at the mining office, Caleb?"

"Just as we thought. Varnes had filed a claim on Lars' mine at the Needles. When I explained the whole situation to Jim, the mining clerk, he simply tore up Varnes' paperwork and put Lars Jensen in as the owner of record."

"That's great. But how'd you get him to do that?"

"He owed me a favor, a big favor," Caleb replied enigmatically. "What happened at the Wells Fargo office?"

Luke started into his story, hesitated, then reached down into his boot and drew out his Wells Fargo badge. "It's time I told everyone here what else I do for a living." Luke then went into an explanation of what he was doing in Durango and why he'd been there. He finished up by recounting the episode with Cecil Thompson and his further suspicions of him.

Caleb shook his head. "I knew you were too good to be true. Looks like I'll be losing a deputy 'fore long."

"And I'll be losing a friend, a good friend," Laura softly added, her eyes welling up.

Luke looked over quickly at Laura. "Not necessarily true on either count. Let's see how this whole thing plays out, Laura. Now that I've come out from undercover, I may have to do something else altogether."

Merv walked in with Rogash and Zeb. Luke looked up at Zeb and raised his eyebrows.

"Hello, Zeb here."

Zeb had been with the Bar H and Dick Hawthorne at the start of the range war with the Circle D a few years before. In fact, Zeb had likely shot the colonel in the first confrontation. Luke had run him out of Kansas instead of killing him.

Zeb looked at Luke, over at Roe and back at Luke. "Aw, I figured sooner or later I'd have to see you Deputy. I'll leave town just as soon as you say."

Luke reflected a moment. "Eddie says you've done some work for him and he's been real satisfied, that right?" In response, Roe mutely nodded, as did Zeb.

"I reckon," Zeb replied. "Since that whole fracas with the Bar H, I stayed on the right side of the law. After hearing what happened to Hawthorne and almost all the rest, I reckon you did me the biggest favor of my life. First by letting me live, then by just running us off. I left Kansas that same night, ain't been back since."

Everyone else had remained silent through this exchange, glancing back and forth between Luke and Zeb. Caleb had a wry grin on his face. "So you were at the Bar H fight?"

"No, no just the first part. I was one of the polecats who bushwhacked the colonel, Luke's pa— thankfully he lived. Luke come back the next day and in a faceoff kilt George Sly, and Sly was the fastest man I ever seen.

"Sly tried to slicker Luke and everthin'. It wasn't even close. Luke offered me the same chance and I don't mind telling you I begged on my knees not to have to take it. Then that there big fellow, Ryan, you kind of remind me of him, Sheriff. Anyways, Ryan, he commenced to give us all a real woodshed kinda' thumpin' and sent us off."

"What have you been doing since?" Caleb asked.

"Oh this'n that. Some mining, ranching, a little gambling, but always on the right side of the law and that's the truth."

Caleb looked over at Luke. "Your call, Luke."

Luke's steel-blue eyes bored into Zeb. "All right, Zeb. You do the job here and maybe you've got yourself a home. Don't do it, or do anything wrong and you'll face me, and I'll be watching you."

"Face you? I'd rather face chained lightning with two sticks of dynamite. I'll do the job, whatever it is. Just you watch."

"I will."

One of the boarders came running in out of breath. "Trouble over at the Wells Fargo office."

Chapter Twenty-eight

Caleb quickly stood up. "Eddie, you, Merv and Rogash stay here and keep watch. Laura, keep your Winchester handy. This may be a trick to draw us off. Zeb, you come with us."

Luke, Caleb and Zeb all hurried to the Wells Fargo office at a dead run. Luke had his Colts, Zeb carried a Winchester and Caleb had retrieved the long Greener shotgun which Luke had given him, from the sheriff's office. The door to the Wells Fargo office stood open. There was a body in the street. It was barely visible through the flurries. *Oh no,* Luke thought, *not Sam. Not now.*

Bystanders were staring at the unmoving body.

One of the onlookers, Charles Cavendish, resplendent in his big buffalo coat, turned and saw Caleb, Zeb and Luke come rushing up. "You boys sure missed it."

"What happened?" Luke asked.

"Well, sir," Cavendish replied maddeningly slow, "he said"—indicating the still form—"'I could crush you like a bug.' And the other fellow said, 'You never could and you never will.' At which point, the other fellow threw a haymaker like Jem Riley, knocked that fellow off his feet, into the snow, and out."

Luke walked up and peered down into the snow. "Why, it's Cecil Thompson."

"No kidding," Caleb said. Zeb said nothing, only looked warily around with a firm grip on his Winchester.

"Sure is," Cavendish said. "Guess he thought he could get back into his office once you were gone, Luke."

Luke glanced at Cavendish. Apparently news traveled fast.

Sam Ball walked out of the office with another hasp to install. "Oh, hi Luke, Sheriff."

"What happened?" Luke, dumbfounded, asked again.

"Oh, it's like I heard Charles say. Cecil wanted

to get back into the office all right and figured since he was twice as big as me he wouldn't have too tough a time."

"I can understand his reasoning," Caleb said.

"Yeah. But when I was in the Army, being the littlest guy in the outfit meant that you had to fight to get just about anything you wanted. I found out that I wasn't too bad at it."

"Apparently not," Luke remarked dryly.

Thompson was starting to stir. He sat up groaning. His jaw was beginning to swell.

"Better keep some of that snow on your jaw, Cecil," Cavendish said. "Looks to me like you been hit with a club."

Thompson staggered to his feet, his hand still on his jaw. Reaching down, he picked up his hat out of the snow and beat it on his leg. He glared at the assemblage, turned and lurched back from whence he had come.

Ball was back at work on the door, whistling a tuneless melody. Luke shook his head, waved at Ball and started back to the Lincoln followed closely by Caleb and Zeb.

Thinking about First Samuel the sixteenth chaptor, Luke said, "You just never know about a body. You have to judge a person on heart, not stature. I won't even think of calling him 'Skinny' again."

"Yep," Caleb agreed, putting it in colloquial perspective, "it ain't the size of the dog in the fight, it's the size of the fight in the dog."

Roe, Rogash and Merv had been keeping a good lookout while Luke, Caleb and Zeb were at the Wells Fargo office. After they all trooped back into the living room, Laura, still carrying her Winchester, came from the back where she'd been watching over Lars.

Mrs. Cray provided more hot coffee and some fresh baked bread, which again was received with many thanks. Then they sat down to work out their strategy and together they came up with a plan.

Leaving the others, Luke, Caleb and Zeb started out from the Lincoln and headed over to Varnes' smelter. They walked up to within forty yards of the entrance spread far apart.

"Varnes!" Caleb called out.

At once a reply came back. "What do you want?"

"I want the bunch of you to throw down your arms and come out here."

A snort came in reply followed by derisive laughter. "Fat chance of that happening. I don't recognize you as sheriff, you're showing too much favoritism."

"If you mean by that I don't like murdering scum, you're right," Caleb again yelled back. "Get out here, now."

"See what I mean," came Varnes' cheeky reply.

The windows of the smelter suddenly bristled with rifles. Caleb cut loose with his shotgun, loaded with buckshot. The deep roar of the double barrels accented the shattering of glass where two of the windows once were only seconds before.

In the same instant, Luke swiftly drew his Colts and shot just inside the window frames where he judged the holders of the weapons might be hiding. Firing with both hands, it was almost like the target range, except that some men might be dying behind those windows. Zeb whipped up his Winchester and fired 17 shots in half as many seconds.

Return fire, at first sporadic, picked up in intensity making close spurts of snow and forcing Luke, Caleb and Zeb to hide behind an outbuilding to reload and regroup. "Well, I think that went real well," Luke said. He was breathing hard, trying to catch his breath.

"Oh yeah," Caleb replied, equally winded. "Any better, and they'd have told us to put glass target balls on top of our heads."

Zeb looked at the two of them as if they had three eyes. With some difficulty, he began shoving shells into the loading gate of his Winchester. His hands were shaking and he was breathing in deep, nervous gasps. The return shots, increasing in volume and hitting the building, sounded like a bored woodpecker that had suddenly taken a renewed interest in its project.

"I think we'd better go back to the Lincoln," Luke said. "I've got an idea that might work a little better than this."

"If it means we don't have to be like ducks in a shooting gallery, I'm all for it," Zeb exclaimed.

Caleb let out a short laugh that sounded more like a bark. "That's okay Zeb, you stood up right well. This was just the first round. If I know Luke, there'll be a better second round."

"Caleb's right, Zeb. I know you were scared. So was I." Zeb looked at Luke in surprise. "That's right. A man would have to be a fool not to be a mite queasy when lead is flying all around him. It's what you do in spite of the fear, not give in to it. And you didn't."

Relief spread over Zeb's face. He'd thought of himself, if not a coward, certainly not a brave man. Yet, with Luke and Caleb standing there trading gunfire with the gang at the smelter, he just couldn't let himself run, at least not until they did. And, he admitted to himself, when they finally did retreat, it wasn't near soon enough for him. Still and all, he'd stuck it out and they'd said he'd done good. And by golly, he felt good.

Chapter Twenty-nine

Back at the Lincoln, they had another meeting.
They decided that Eddie Roe would go to the Wells
Fargo office to back up Sam Ball. Also, Roe might
be able to recruit some help from the Lucky Dog, if
needed. Rogash, a Civil War veteran, would stay
with Laura to help guard Lars, and Merv would go
back with Luke, Caleb and Zeb to the smelter. All
the helpers, including Ball, would be designated
special deputies in case there was any doubt about
the legality of the situation.

A long telegram from Jerome Puddington was
delivered to Luke. He was surprised that the response came so quickly. When he saw the contents,

154

he knew why. It appeared that in about seventy-five percent of the stage robberies Cecil Thompson had known, or could have found out, what the contents of the shipments were. That was too high a percentage to just be coincidental. They'd go after Thompson too. Confirming that point, Ball rushed in followed closely by Roe.

"Luke, I thought you should see this. I found a ledger hidden in a secret compartment in Cecil's desk. It shows how he'd give out correct deposit slips then siphon off money from accounts of people he knew were going to stay here. As long as they were here, he'd move the money around to cover any withdrawals."

"But," Luke continued the thought, "with the interest Wells Fargo pays, four percent every half-year, chances are they'd leave the money in their accounts."

"Exactly. It appears that old Cecil was setting himself up for a big payday."

Laura had come out front from her dad's room. "That explains why he didn't want to show me anything about my Dad."

"Right," Luke said. "It also appears that Thompson and Varnes were in cahoots on those stage robberies."

Caleb laughed. "Along with seein' stars, old Cecil

must have seen dollar signs floating away, when Sam coldcocked him."

Luke had a sudden thought. "Who's at the Wells Fargo office?"

Roe interjected. "Bob Cromwell happened in, and I put him over there. We thought this situation was too important not to let you know about it immediately."

"Good. Sam, send a wire to Jerome Puddington outlining everything you've found. Tell him we're going after Cecil Thompson and Varnes. Sign it with your name as station manager. Jerome might as well get to know who you are."

"Right away, Luke." Ball beamed as he rushed out the door.

"I think you've found a new friend, Luke," Caleb said.

"He's worth his weight in gold, to Wells Fargo and to me." Luke knew his remark would make the rounds in this small town and he was glad. "All right, let's get back to the smelter."

Caleb was right about round two. Luke took his Sharps, and Caleb and Zeb took the Springfields, which they had retrieved from the two bushwhackers up in the rocks. While all these rifles were single shot and the Springfields were slow to load, they represented much more of a threat to an entrenched, fortified group. The cartridges were long and powerful, particularly the Sharps, and their bullets could penetrate far deeper than the standard .44-40 Winchester bullet.

Luke stood behind the outbuilding, Caleb got behind some barrels of rainwater which had frozen solid, and Zeb stood far out on the other side. Zeb was out of the direct line of fire, but was to harass the bunch in the smelter with rifle fire directed at the side of the smelter. Roe and Merv were also out to the side, armed with Winchesters.

There weren't quite as many rifles at the windows of the smelter as there were before. Nonetheless they were menacing.

Deliberately, Luke shot through the wall of the smelter and his big Sharps reverberated in the enclosed area. Caleb and Zeb followed suit. While they were met with sporadic return fire, it was not well aimed. Clearly, no one wanted to be anywhere near the windows or even stand up in the building. The whole place was a hazardous area. Luke fired several more rounds, stitching a pattern in the smelter building wall, like a trickshot punching out a playing card.

There were yells and howls coming from the

smelter. Suddenly, a white sheet tied to the barrel of a Winchester was seen waving back and forth out of one of the shattered windows.

"Throw out all your weapons!" Caleb yelled. "Then come on out, one at a time with your hands held high!"

"Leave your dead and wounded!" Luke added. "We'll get them later."

An assortment of rifles and handguns came flying out the windows. The snow muffled any sounds they made as they hit the ground. A slow procession of five walked out of the smelter. The last one was bent over holding his shoulder, blood running down his sleeve.

The first man in line was a gaunt, tall man with a dark tobacco-stained beard. His eyes were black and had a haunted, wild look. He had a slouch hat tied onto his head with a scarf and his mackinaw was buttoned up to his chin. His hands were held high and he was shivering.

"Mmmmy–y–y name's Avery, Roger Avery."

"Where's Varnes and the rest?" Caleb asked.

"Th–they lit a shuck out of here, right after you fellows quit shootin' the first time."

"Then why'd you continue to shoot when we came back?" Luke wanted to know.

"Varnes offered us one thousand dollars each if

we could hold you fer–fer six hours, then we could surrender. When them big slugs started goin' through the walls like they was paper, we decided we couldn't collect no one thousand dollars if we was all dead. Baldwin was propped up, sitting clear in the back drinking coffee, when a slug caught him right in the brisket. Went through three walls it did. You done kil't another one too."

Luke had a small smile. "Looks like this just wasn't Baldwin's town. First he tried to kill me. Then Caleb shot him. Now I guess he's gone for good."

"Which way did they go?" Caleb asked, surpressing a smile himself.

"S–s–south. I think Riley h–h–had a stop to make first, then he was gonna catch up to them."

A cold stab of fear hit Luke like a dagger thrust. He whirled and broke into a dead run. He yelled over his shoulder, "Caleb, I'll see you at the jail. Eddie, come on."

Chapter Thirty

Laura was sitting back with Lars, talking softly to him, when she heard a crash in the front room. She rushed out with a Colt revolver in her hand and saw Rogash prone on the floor, bleeding. From the side stepped Jem Riley, who plucked the Colt from her hand and put it behind him, in his belt. He grabbed Laura around the waist with his right hand and Laura screamed.

Riley laughed. "We got us a little unfinished business, missy. Where's your coat, it's gonna be cold."

Lars hobbled out from the back bedroom, his cane making a slow tap–tap on the hardwood floor. When he saw Laura in the grasp of Riley, he started forward with his cane raised to strike. Riley laughed again, and with the back of his left hand he knocked Lars down. "It's gonna cost ya one hundred thousand dollars to get this little filly back in one piece." Then Riley took another swipe at Lars and knocked him unconscious.

While Riley was beating her father, Laura reached into one of her dress pockets and came up with a Remington double-barreled derringer in her left hand. While still in Riley's grasp, she pointed it back over her shoulder and shoved it into Riley's armpit and fired. The noise was loud in her ear. Riley let go of Laura as fast as if she'd suddenly turned into a mountain lion. He grabbed his left armpit, which felt as if it had been struck by a rattlesnake.

"Why—you." Riley started toward Laura. He had his fist cocked back. He was going to take her head off with one swing.

Laura fired again. This time she hit Riley in the stomach with a stubby little bullet. Riley backed up a half a step, he looked down at his stomach in wonderment, he stared at Laura, then started toward her again.

Laura put the empty derringer in one skirt pocket and from the other pocket she pulled out another derringer. From five feet she couldn't miss and she didn't.

Taking careful aim she hit Riley right between the eyes. If it had been anyone else that would have ended the altercation. This time however, the bullet broke the skin and instead of breaking his thick skull, the skull that had broken the hands of so many unwary opponents, it traveled around it inside the skin and exited just behind Riley's ear. Riley, stunned, took another lurching step forward.

Laura calmly shot him again, this time in the chest. Riley backed up, sat down and leaned against the wall.

His eyelids fluttered and he was breathing in short gasps. Laura eyed him warily as she pulled the little side lever of the pistol and flipped the barrels up. She ejected the two empty cartridge casings and reloaded with fresh shells. She repeated this process with the other pistol.

Hearing shots fired, Mrs. Cray came out from the back with a shotgun, and she leveled it at Riley. Laura cocked the hammers of both her little pistols and also leveled them at Riley.

Riley seemed to be in no condition to argue at the turn of events. With Roe running a far distant second, Luke came rushing in through the front door, his pistols drawn. He was astonished at the spectacle before him. "Laura, Mrs. Cray, are you all right?"

Mrs Cray answered first. "That's one brave girl there, Luke Dawson. I came out after everything was all over."

"Laura?" Luke asked softly.

Laura didn't take her eyes off Riley, and kept her pistols trained on him.

"Please, see to my dad and Rogash, Luke."

Luke easily picked up the unconscious Lars Jensen and carried him to his room. Lars was a little worse for wear but his breathing was normal. Mrs. Cray followed them back. Next, he checked on Rogash who was bleeding from a nasty head wound. Luke bound up the wound and also got Rogash to a bed with Roe's help.

When he came out, Riley was making an effort to talk. His teeth were clenched against the pain and blood was seeping into one eye from his head wound.

"Dawson," Riley gasped through gritted teeth, "Dawson."

Luke walked over and crouched down so he could hear Riley. "Riley, you sure are a mess," Luke said without sympathy.

"Dawson. Shoot . . . me."

"What?" Luke asked, wondering if he'd heard correctly.

"Shoot . . . me."

"Well, as tempting as that sounds, why should I?"

"I don't never want it said that Jem Riley was killed by no . . . girl. Them little popguns of hers ain't done the job . . . yet."

"Riley, you take the cake. You really do. You'd rather be killed for sure by me, instead of hanging onto a slim chance that you might recover from being shot by a girl?"

"That's . . . right."

"Well, much as it pains me, I'm not going to accommodate you. I don't cotton much to murder, even of a skunk like you. Cheer up though, you might die after all, and if Lars or Rogash die, we'll hang you anyway."

Riley started to lapse into unconsciousness. Luke grabbed him by the left arm. Riley started awake with the pain. "Riley, hey, Riley. Where were you going to meet Varnes and Biggs?"

Riley looked at Luke through threequarter shut eyes. "Down at the ruins—the fat man was with them too."

"Thompson? Sure, that makes sense. I reckon this town was getting too hot for him. He was the one that gave you and Varnes the information on what stages to hit, wasn't he?"

Riley weakly nodded his head.

"You were the third man in the stage robberies too, weren't you?"

Riley stared dully at Luke.

"You might as well tell me Riley, you're likely to die anyway. It'll do you good to get it off your chest."

Riley slowly nodded, twice.

"Riley, you ever kill anybody?"

"Not . . . that I know of. Not–not outside the . . . ring." Riley's head lolled over to the side.

"All right, Riley," Luke continued in his maddeningly cheerful voice. "We'll go ahead and dig the lead out of you. Probably at the worst, we'll save you for the hangman."

Riley, didn't hear the last part, he had passed out.

"Luke," Laura said softly.

Luke turned around, "Laura, are you all right? I didn't even think to ask again, you looked so formidable with those two pistols."

"I'm fine." Indicating Riley, she said, "He's got a Colt stuck in the back of his belt, he took it from me."

"And that's all the weapons that he thought you had?" Luke asked.

Laura nodded. Luke retrieved the pistol and gave it back to her.

Roe had followed Luke into the Lincoln and

was awed at how Riley had come out second in his scrap with Laura. He just kept staring at Riley's massive frame, lying there inert.

"Laura," Luke gently asked again, "are you sure you're all right?"

Laura, in a very subdued manner, nodded. "It's just that I've never done anything like that before. Do you think I killed him?"

"Laura, honey, if ever a man needed killin' this one is first in line. I'm just thankful that you had the presence of mind to act the way you did. If I had the time, I wouldn't mind practicing some doctoring on old Jem there. It wouldn't much bother me which way it went."

Roe chuckled and Laura fleetingly smiled for the first time that day.

Chapter Thirty-one

"I've got to get over to the jail and see Caleb. Maybe we can catch Varnes, Thompson and Biggs before they get too far. They'll be expecting Riley and they're far short of the six-hour start they wanted. I'll send a few people back to fetch Riley. Eddie, would you stay and guard Laura? Or maybe," Luke said on reflection, "Laura, would you stay here and guard Eddie?" All three of them chuckled.

Luke retrieved his Sharps, got his big dun saddled and raced over to the jail. He explained hurriedly to Caleb what had happened at the Lincoln, and Riley's subsequent confession. Caleb dispatched a wagon to get Riley and sent for Clancy to check on Lars and Rogash. Then he asked for Clancy to come back to do some "lead mining" on Riley.

Sam Ball walked in as Luke was telling what happened, and listened with rapt attention. "Four times, she shot him four times? I've known of men who were killed with just one shot from a .41."

"It isn't like she wasn't tryin', particularly with that head shot, but Riley's not out of the woods yet. Cromwell at the office?

"Yeah, he's tolerable tough, and big enough to kill a bear with a switch. I may want to keep him around as a door stop," Ball answered. Luke laughed.

Puzzled, Caleb asked, "Riley really wanted you to shoot him because he didn't want to be killed by a girl?"

"Yep. It's almost like out of the Old Testament where this old boy was besieging a town and a woman dropped a big stone on his head. He had his armor bearer kill him so it wouldn't be known he was killed by a woman."

"Do you think Riley was thinking about that when he asked you to kill him?" Caleb asked.

"I don't think so." Luke laughed, everyone else joined in.

Ball insisted on joining the hunt for Cecil and the rest. "I'm sure he's got some stolen Wells

Fargo money with him. He's also got to pay for tipping off Varnes and his gang about those stage shipments. He owes Wells Fargo and I owe him."

"I think you gave him a down payment already," Luke wryly observed.

"All right," Caleb said. "Let's gather up some supplies, weapons, warm gear and food. We don't know how long we're going to be out on the hunt. We'll meet over at the Lincoln in forty-five minutes."

There were four of them gathered in front of Lincoln House—Zeb decided to go with them too.

Mrs. Cray packed all the biscuits she had, along with some fresh churned butter, some beef and some canned peaches. "No reason why you boys shouldn't eat well, for a few days anyway."

Thanks were heartfelt from all four riders. Laura had donned her sheepskin coat and came out to see Luke off. She threw her arms around him and kissed him. "Please be careful, Luke. These men you're going after are killers of the worst kind."

Luke was pleasantly surprised at this unexpected display of affection and enthusiastically kissed her back. "I'll be back, but I won't forget that they were going to try to use you for money and their freedom. Don't worry, we'll be careful."

The weather was still bone-chilling cold but the snow, though deep, was coming down only in dancing flurries not like the blinding blizzard earlier. They made twenty miles that first day and continued long into the evening.

After building a shelter, and enjoying a hot meal thanks to Mrs. Cray, they settled in for the night wrapped in their buffalo robes. The wind howled, and the low fire crackled, giving off the scent of freshly burned pine. They traded shifts on guard duty, with Luke taking the first.

At first light, they were up and on the trail again. The going, while not easy, was at least made more tolerable since they were following the stage road.

"How far to the ruins?" Zeb asked.

"About another forty miles," Luke said.

Ten miles out the second day, Caleb spotted a telltale lump, partially hidden in the snow not far off the main trail. They all rode over and dismounted to inspect it further. "Good thing the wind was up and the snow was down," Zeb observed. "Elsewise, we never woulda seen whatever it is."

The body was lying face down, hands outstretched, like a kid diving in the snow. There were two bullet holes, close together in the back.

Luke reached down and grabbed a shoulder and turned the body over slowly. He stared into the sightless eyes of former Wells Fargo manager Cecil Thompson.

"I guess Cecil overestimated his importance to Varnes," Caleb commented.

"Yep," Luke said. "Cecil didn't know he'd become a liability."

"A liability?" Ball asked.

"Sure," Luke continued. "He'd been fired from Wells Fargo, blacklisted among other express agencies, so he couldn't do Varnes any good when he set up operations somewhere else. Couple that with an extra horse that Varnes probably needed."

"Why would he need an extra horse?" Zeb wondered.

"I'm sure Varnes loaded up with all the pure gold from his smelter that he could carry, without worrying who it rightfully belonged to. Likely he needed the packing space."

"Plus," Ball added, "Cecil still got away with a lot of money that belonged to Wells Fargo."

"We're not likely to find any of it on him now," Caleb said. And they didn't.

They pushed farther on—the only consolation was that Varnes and Biggs were going through the same weather, fleeing with just as much difficulty as their chasers. That evening they camped just five miles short of the ruins.

"How long do you think they'll stay at the ruins?" Ball asked.

"Half a day, a day at the outside," Caleb replied.

"That short?" Luke asked.

"Sure. They expect to see Riley and Laura coming in. While it would be slower going with Laura, they won't think he's far behind. If Riley doesn't show up in quick time, or if they spot us, they are goin' to hightail it. Then we'll play hob tryin' to find 'em."

"Do you think they've got a spyglass?" Luke asked.

"I wouldn't count on them not having one, why?"

"I was thinking we could give them exactly what they are expecting to see."

"You mean Riley and Laura?" Zeb asked.

"Exactly."

"How?" Ball asked. Then he realized something and said, "Wait a minute."

Caleb and Luke started to chuckle, Zeb was still puzzled.

Luke, still chuckling, said, "No offense Sam but you are about the same size as Laura. I'm probably a couple inches shorter than Riley, while Caleb is a little bigger so it's probably a toss up as to which one of us goes with you. What we have to do is bind up our faces with scarves, and whoever plays Riley will have to wrap one around his head to cover up the area which should be bald."

They flipped a coin and Caleb won. He got to play Riley. Luke deployed Zeb in a huge semi-circle going south, and he went north. They stayed well out of sight of the ruins so as not to be spotted, even if Varnes had a glass. The wind was increasing from a howl to almost a gale.

Snow continued to fall but only lightly, and when it hit exposed flesh it was with the force of needles. At the signal hour of 10 A.M., Caleb started out, leading Ball's horse toward the ruins. The driving wind made them both keep their heads down.

Homer Biggs was the first to spot the riders. "Here they come, I can't believe Riley pulled it off."

Varnes put Cecil Thompson's binoculars up to his eyes and smiled, showing his gold teeth on the right side of his face. "I knew he could, he hates Dawson almost as much as I do. We'll get all of Jensen's gold yet, most of it anyway."

Biggs asked, "How much do you need Riley now that you've got the girl?"

"Riley has his uses. He's tough as nails and meaner'n a snake. I think there's still some money to be made in prize fightin' him."

"That girl sure looks reluctant."

"She's a feisty one, we'll take the starch out of her," Varnes answered.

Chapter Thirty-two

A sudden gust of wind tore Caleb's hat off of his head, exposing the scarf underneath along with some hair.

"Hey," Varnes yelled, "that's not Riley, Riley's bald. It looks like that big sheriff. Get 'em."

Biggs opened fire with his Winchester and Varnes followed suit. Caleb was shot out of the saddle with the first volley. Ball hunkered down and finally dismounted rather than be a sitting duck. He went over to check on Caleb. Caleb had been shot low on the left side—he was conscious but in pain and shock was surely setting in.

Ball half-dragged and half-carried Caleb behind

a low rock outcropping just off the trail. He had to keep bent double to avoid the bullets ricocheting around him off the rocks. Ball ran back and retrieved the Winchester from Caleb's saddle scabbard. The spurts of snow from the bullets coming in were quickly swept away by the ferocious wind.

Luke and Zeb were closing in on Varnes and Biggs from opposite directions. The sound of gunfire was pretty well drowned out by the screaming wind. Nevertheless, when Luke saw Biggs and Varnes firing into the distance he didn't hesitate.

Bringing up his Winchester, he let off a fusillade of rifle fire. Biggs did a pirouette and then a dance like a puppet on a string before he collapsed in the snow.

Zeb opened up from the other side, contributing to the assault. Varnes threw his rifle over the rocks and dropped down. He reached back up showing both hands above the rocks and began to wave them in surrender. Luke and Zeb closed in to disarm him.

"Don't shoot, don't shoot," Varnes screamed into the wind. "I can explain everything."

Luke put Zeb to guarding Varnes and went back to check on Caleb. "We've got to get him to a cave in the ruins. It'll be better than camping out in the snow," Luke yelled into the wind. Ball nodded vigorously.

They managed to get Caleb onto his horse and then slowly led it into the ruins. Luke went and got the packhorses and brought them up. They took the buffalo robes and made Caleb as comfortable as possible. The cave was set back with shelter on three sides and the wind couldn't penetrate. Luke went to the woods and grubbed for some roots and plants, and Ball cut wood for a fire. Caleb was still conscious—fortunately the bullet had gone clear through his side.

When they got back Zeb said, "This one's real cute." He indicated Varnes with his Colt. "He tried to buy his way out of here by offering me money to let him skedadle. Said you'd have to look after Caleb and it'd work."

Varnes smiled, his easy confidence was coming back. "No such thing, I was just making a hypothetical business proposition. You want to talk about Thompson? That was all Biggs. Fact is, I got a lawyer up Denver way that'll make any charges against me look like so much child's play. Why, with enough money spread around I may not even come to trial. I'll just—"

There was an explosion, extremely loud in the enclosed space. Acrid smoke was curling up from the .44-40 Colt, then whisked away in the swirling air. Varnes had a surprised expression on his face as he slowly toppled over, spasmodically jerked twice then lay still.

Zeb looked around, everyone had shocked expressions. "That's the first true thing old Varnes said today, about not coming to trial. It's nice he could go out on a true statement." Zeb calmly reloaded his Colt then holstered it.

"Why Zeb?" Luke asked.

"When I first come down here, I ran across Ole and Gus at their diggin's. They took me in, treated me right. I ran a few errands for 'em, they didn't much like to come into town. They was nice men, I liked them, they deserved better. I was afraid that old Varnes just might slither out of everthin' he done. I guess I'm sorry Luke."

Luke thought about that phrase *deserved better.* He'd heard it before, and it applied here. "Don't be sorry, I was thinking about hanging him anyway."

"Oh, I ain't sorry I kilt him, just fer any trouble it might cause you. Knowing what he did to Gus and Ole, well, I just got tired all over of listenin' to him."

Chapter Thirty-three

After the initial surprise at the gunshot, Caleb closed his eyes and lay back into his robes.

Ball looked at Zeb and said, "Well, if anyone was goin' to do it, I'm glad it was you."

Zeb looked back at Ball and Luke with a small smile. "That was my figgerin' too, Sam. Caleb is the law, and you're Wells Fargo, and Luke, well, he's both, you're all real upstandin' folk. Me? I'm just a driftin' hombre who got scared on to the right side of the law back in Kansas. Stayed there too, 'til now that is. I didn't figger it'd matter much if I was the one who give some quick justice. Hope there ain't no trouble about it. But I've had trouble before."

179

"You know what, Zeb," Luke said. "We're way outside the jurisdiction of Durango. I don't think there'll be any trouble with Caleb, I know there won't with me. And speaking for Wells Fargo, I can say that they'll be so glad to get their stolen money back that they'll pay a reward, at least five hundred dollars. That right, Mr. Station Manager?"

"That's exactly right Luke," Sam chimed in.

"Well I swan," said a smiling Zeb. "Ain't it great, when you stay on the right side of the law?"

Chapter Thirty-four

After another day Caleb was well enough to travel. They'd put Biggs and Varnes in a common shallow grave near the ruins. The bullion and money and supplies were fastened on the remaining horses. Three days of travel later they made quite a procession coming into Durango.

On the way back, Luke was lost in thought. He wasn't sure which way he would go, from Durango. He'd done what he'd been sent there to do—solve the stage holdups. In the process, he'd uncovered a corrupt Wells Fargo manager and hired a darned good one. He knew any decision he made on his future wouldn't concern just him. He knew that for certain when they rode in and stopped at the front of the Lincoln House.

There at the window was Laura.

Heedless of the biting cold, she rushed out the door and into Luke's arms. He knew, for him, there would never be anyone else.